THE MACHINE

by

M. S. VALENTINE

CHIMERA

The Martinet first published in 2002 by
Chimera Publishing Ltd
PO Box 152
Waterlooville
Hants
PO8 9FS

Printed and bound in Great Britain by
Cox & Wyman Ltd, Reading.

This book is sold subject to the condition that it shall not, by
way of trade or otherwise, be lent, resold, hired out or
otherwise circulated without the publisher's prior written
consent in any form of binding or cover other than that in
which it is published, and without a similar condition being
imposed on the subsequent purchaser.

The characters and situations in this book are entirely
imaginary and bear no relation to any real person or actual
happening.

Copyright © M. S. Valentine

The right of M. S. Valentine to be identified as author of this book has been asserted in
accordance with section 77 and 78 of the Copyrights Designs and Patents Act 1988

THE MARTINET

M. S. Valentine

This novel is fiction – in real life practice safe sex

Martinet *(mär'tn-et')* *n. 1. A strict disciplinarian. 2. A person who demands absolute adherence to methods or rules.*

Foreword

Justice can be cruel. In fact, it usually is for those to whom justice has been meted out. However, in its cruelty there might be room for negotiation. Indeed, the seemingly unyielding individuals who hand down the rule of law may elect to exercise considerable discretion in their duties. As for the apprehensive individuals who stand trembling before those in authority because they have gone awry in their deeds, they need not watch despairingly as the springtime of their lives turns into winter. For there *are* alternatives.

As a general rule, those who misbehave according to the rules and dictates of society are sent either to a penal colony or, depending upon how a particular administrator of justice might choose to evaluate the situation, to another less harsh place; a place where they will learn discipline; a place where they will be kept under the strict control and supervision of one who knows best how to curtail the occasional errant criminal urge, or leastwise to channel such urges into those of a more favourable kind.

It is in this place where these petty pilferers – as well as those of aristocratic blood whose actions place them in bad stead with their families – will come to be ruled by the Martinet.

The Castle

In the distant past, the place known only as the Castle sat majestically atop a craggy knoll overlooking a dry and scrubby landscape that to this day continues to bear no name. Alas, the Castle has now become little more than a tragic ruin, the illicit goings-on that so freely transpired on a daily basis behind its thick stone walls the stuff of idle speculation by historians and peasant talebearers alike. This Moorish remain belongs not to the legal boundaries of Cordoba, or even to those of Sevilla, but instead occupies a sun baked wasteland of its very own. Perhaps these great cities of Spain wished not to lay claim to this formerly imposing structure. Not that the city rulers could be blamed for this unusual lapse of proprietorship. Even those in ignorance of the Castle's true function thought it wiser to ignore this decaying monument to a cruel and tarnished past in the hope its fallen archways and collapsed domes might vanish completely over time, leaving the land clean and clear and ready for what would surely be a much needed redemption.

This is a place rarely spoken of by locals, who understand little of the man who once lived there and still less of the activities that transpired within these mysterious frontiers. Imposing in its Moorish austerity, the structure has been the cause of much fear and conjecture over the centuries. It was constructed in the *Caliphal* style of architecture, although undoubtedly its nomadic builders could never have conceived of the use to which this formidable edifice would one day be put. If a traveller were to visit this part of Spain today, he or she could easily locate the crumbling remains of the Castle when traversing the craggy wilderness between Cordoba and Sevilla. As the pious might choose to make a pilgrimage to the Mezquita, those whose tastes run towards the less sacrosanct might choose to pay homage to the enigmatic man who, until the day of his death – and some claim thereafter in the belief that his fleshly remains have intermingled with those of his stone dwelling – lived within the Castle walls, a man known only as the Martinet. Even in these jaded modern times he is still greatly admired and emulated, and his practices continue to be carried on, centuries after his demise, by secret societies around the globe.

Not a lot has changed in this region since the Martinet reigned over his self-made kingdom, although today this sunny southern Spanish landscape tends to be more populated by olives than by living beings of the flesh-and-blood variety. For in days past, one would have needed to gain access to the Castle to pass through the land surrounding it, and access to the Castle, with the sole exception of those who had the misfortune of being sent to the Martinet as punishment, was by strict invitation only. Only the most privileged of individuals would be allowed to pass through the Castle's strictly guarded gates to partake of the exotic fare on offer within its walls, fare the most licentious of souls would have been at a loss to find in their societies, no matter how decadent or hedonistic. On any given evening, one might even encounter a member of royalty, and more often than not without being aware of having done so. The king of Spain himself made a frequent habit of calling at the Castle, as did the rulers of other powerful kingdoms, all of whom hid their imperial façades behind a mask. Be that as it may, for some this accessory might easily have been done without, the often quite distinctive features of their wearers proving all but impossible to disguise, as in the case of the Spanish king, whose formidable physique and equally impressive member would be immediately recognised by all and sundry.

News of the arrival of the great and mighty king would inspire the Martinet's charmingly masked lady guests to powder their ample and sweetly scented bosoms in the unlikely event his highness would decide to turn his fancy toward one not of the domestic female variety and, in so doing, take up the challenge of exploring beneath her aristocratic panniers, since it had been rumoured a vacancy in the queen's chambers was forthcoming. Indeed, the prodigious king could have taken his pick of lovely ladies at court, a practice he was all too quickly tiring of despite the occasional amusement of procuring a rival's wife or, in some instances, a rival's son. Yet it was the young, yielding bodies of the Castle slaves the king of Spain desired most, a desire eagerly shared by the very same ladies whose fluttering eyelashes and perfumed bosoms the king pointedly ignored. For there were nearly as many female guests staying at the Castle as there were male guests, an unusual occurrence in itself considering the gruelling nature and great distance of the journey to this notoriously dangerous region of Spain. It was not unheard of for a coach to be robbed along the dusty roadside, or for its female passengers to be abducted by ruthless bands of highwaymen who might show their charity by setting their victims free after they had thoroughly enjoyed them. Nevertheless, even such well known risks made not a bit of difference to these determined ladies of title, for the pleasures awaiting them at the Castle outweighed any hazards that may have hindered them in their quest.

It might be thought the Martinet had designed the Castle for the sole purpose of enticing these corseted ladies of the court into its erotic embrace rather than leaving such architectural matters to the past ingenuity of the Moors. For although the skirts of the day extended out nearly four feet at the sides, rarely did a lady display the slightest difficulty entering or leaving a room or sitting in a chair. The doorways had been constructed especially wide by their Saracen builders, accommodating the fashion of later centuries and the prevailing style in chairs, whose absence of armrests allowed a lady to seat herself unhampered and without clumsiness. As for the gentlemen, their cutaway coats draped easily down the sides of their chairs, offering little in the way of wrinkling but offering much in the way of convenience when being serviced by a slave, as they needed only to unlace the front of their breeches to be pleasured. It mattered not whether a gentleman of the nobility was in the midst of enjoying a tasty supper of cold soup and cured ham or even a fine ragout of oxtail. Nor did it matter that those seated around him at table were his social peers – a gentleman's needs had to be met, as did those of a lady. Many an elegant skirt could be seen to have suddenly taken life from the bobbing head sequestered with slavish duty beneath it. Indeed, the privileged of Europe found themselves even more privileged under the Martinet's multi-domed roof.

Fortunately, there was no shortage of appealing young men and women forced by their sentences of servitude to contribute to these aristocrats' sense of privilege. For the Martinet's slaves did not consist merely of petty thieves brought before the law. Although the occasional sticky-fingered servant could be found residing within the Castle's stone walls, so too could the unruly daughter or son of a titled family. In fact, more often than not, a guest would encounter the latter, whose distinguished pedigrees remained safely hidden by the humiliating bonds of their enslavement. There were no class distinctions at the Castle. Whether lowly scullery maid or genteel viscount, all were treated the same, just as they were ruled the same. Punishment was punishment. The man before whom these individuals had been forced to assemble could not allow himself to be impressed by the blueness of their blood.

Be it guest or humble slave, those among the specially selected to enter the Castle gates took an oath of secrecy never to reveal what they had seen and experienced during their stay. Of course, this rule was frequently broken in stylish drawing rooms and parlours all throughout Europe judging by the increasing number of nobility begging an invitation from the Martinet. As for the slaves who eventually left this imposing structure of rock and marble and creeping ivy, they did not dare tell of their experiences, for the lessons mastered could not so easily be unlearned or spoken of. Nevertheless, even if these former slaves chose to speak openly of their experiences, it was highly unlikely they were ever believed.

The Castle's departing slaves whispered their shameful secrets to the sparkling waters of the Guadalquivir as their coaches and carts took them back over the Puente Romano bridge and back to the lives they had left behind, lives which, depending upon their station, consisted either of the requisite duties of the aristocracy or the tedium of performing chores for the aristocracy. Perhaps this explained why some dispatched to the Martinet for punishment chose to remain behind with him rather than return to a life of domestic dreariness, a life of emptying chamber pots and sweeping floors and plucking foul. Living beneath the iron thumb of the man who reigned supreme at the Castle was by no means a lazy existence, however, and some found themselves so altered by the experience they could not live any other way afterwards, so successful had been their indoctrination. The imprints left by the bands of hide at their waists, and the piercings in their most tender parts, were symbols of domination that could not easily be erased.

The Martinet

The Martinet wielded his ivory-headed walking stick at the Castle with absolute authority. Respected by his guests and feared in equal measure by his slaves, the ruler of the Castle seldom bore witness to the wanton transactions taking place between those he invited into his home and those whose youthful folly had placed them there in residence. The Martinet had full knowledge of what transpired beneath his crenulated roof, and therefore he considered his presence at the actual events superfluous. In his mind, it was more important that his aristocratic guests freely and unabashedly enjoy his unique form of hospitality than for his own personal prurience to be satisfied.

A gentleman of great mystery, the Martinet had never been known to show his face. Not even the slaves who remained with him the longest ever caught him unawares, let alone the occasional lady of title with whom he intimately involved himself. It immediately became apparent to all who encountered the Castle proprietor that he possessed a natural attractiveness, a quality that made him the subject of much erotic speculation. However, few could ever hope to curry their host's sexual favours. A busy man, the Martinet preferred to satisfy his physical needs with one of his slaves rather than complicate matters with a guest, which would inevitably lead to gossip and tears, not to mention bitter recriminations. One experience dwelling in the house of love had been enough for him, just as it had been for the many distinguished visitors who asked only for the easily satisfied and uncomplicated passions his home provided.

Like those enslaved at the Castle and those who were frequent callers to it, the Martinet also sought out the safety and anonymity of a mask, concealing his refined features behind a hand stitched piece of rare Oriental silk stiffened with bees' wax and attached around his head by a length of gold cord. Whether for daily wear or for festive occasions, the silk used in the construction of his face masks was always a lustrous royal blue, a colour that matched his eyes to perfection and became known as his trademark. Neither guest nor slave would have dared to don a mask of an equivalent shade, although a full spectrum of colours was made available to the former, many of whom went to great expense ordering their masks from the same Paris milliner as their host. Beneath his mask, only the Martinet's eyes and lips could be seen, eyes that glowed hot with an otherworldly fire and lips that brimmed with a never sated lust. Any facial flesh left exposed to view presented itself as smooth and without flaw, leaving no clue as to the age of the person concealed behind this elegant shield of blue.

In the matter of his true identity, many theories have been put forth, the most accepted being that the Martinet was of royal blood. It has even been rumoured he was descended from the Visigoth king, Pelayo, who defeated the Moors in the eighth century, which would explain how the Castle came into his possession in the first place. It has likewise been rumoured that he took the Spanish throne after Napoleon's humiliating defeat at Waterloo, ruling his subjects with rigid absolutism, the same rigid absolutism with which he had ruled his slaves. But only the Martinet himself could put an end to all the mystery surrounding his identity, and he has long since been dead, although surely not forgotten.

Those who came to hear of the Castle did so via a secret grapevine, which twisted its sensual way through Europe's greatest countries and through Europe's greatest monarchies, reaching across the cold treacherous waters of the Channel to the palaces and manor houses of England. As word spread, the Martinet found himself attracting a series of steady devotees of unusual sophistication and tastes. Be it duke, marquis, viscount or even king, all called upon the Martinet to partake of the fleshly pleasures he placed on offer. And such pleasures were multitude, with not even the most socially forbidden tastes denied. Indeed, their enigmatic host actually seemed to encourage the illicit and was therefore considered by his guests as most magnanimous when it came to overlooking personal foibles. Had he wished to, the Martinet could have embarked upon a lucrative career of blackmail, since his guests held important positions in society and in the government. However, the simple act of extorting money and riches from those with a good deal of it to spare was not the Martinet's intention. On the contrary, he desired only for his guests to indulge themselves without restraint... unless, of course, restraints were what a guest preferred.

As for the Martinet and his physical needs, no one had ever observed him engaging in a tryst with any of his slaves, let alone the masked and high-born personages of the ladies and gentlemen who came to the Castle in search of fleshly satisfaction. Yet surely their inscrutable host could not have been immune to the pleasures of the flesh. Perhaps he secreted his desires behind locked doors, unlike his oftentimes base guests, who indulged quite freely and openly and with little thought toward making themselves the objects of lascivious entertainment for their privileged peers. Undoubtedly, the convenient anonymity of their masks allowed for so much unbridled activity to take place, since no one could ever be certain as to the identity of those observed in such delicious *flagrante delicto*. The presence of others of similar ilk added significantly to the enjoyment of these aristocratic pursuers of pleasure. At any hour of the day or night, a noble gentleman could be spied with his blissfully ungoverned member ramming aggressively into the forcefully prized buttocks of a female slave or even that of a male slave, just as a lady of the nobility might be glimpsed with the head of a slave taking shelter beneath her crinolines, those of the female variety being the most preferred since they were also the most forbidden.

But perhaps the most forbidden of fruits came in the handsome figure of their host, whose dispassionate demeanour many noblewomen tried to disturb. Despite the enslaved presence of so many desirable specimens of both genders ready to perform anyone's sexual bidding at the mere crook of a finger, many prepossessing ladies of title endeavoured to engage their host's attentions, for surely he preferred the perfumed orifices of a marchioness to those of some ill-bred commoner. They would happily have offered the shapely cushions of their bottoms to his ivory-headed walking stick had he so desired to place his mark upon them. If the Martinet ever became aware of these frequently bold and, in his view, embarrassing attempts to gain his notice, he made no effort to acquiesce to them. In fact, he had long ago abandoned his elegant walking stick as a means of coercion, its presence now serving only as an affectation. Unfortunately, this seeming lack of interest on his part did not always preclude further attempts to gain his attention by the fine ladies who frequented his home.

Never in all his days at the Castle did the Martinet forget a certain foreign countess's flagrant efforts to gain his favours. Under the pretext of having misplaced her valuable diamond aigrette, the countess sought out her masked host far and away from the eyes and ears of her peers, one of whom happened to be her husband. The Martinet could both see and hear the lady's determined approach. The torches burning in their iron sconces on the walls of the corridor illuminated her progress toward the partially open door of his bedchamber, the reverberant acoustics of her equally determined footfalls against the stone floor increasing in volume and serving as an alarm call for the room's solitary occupant. It was unheard of for a guest to go anywhere near the Martinet's private apartments. Nevertheless, it soon became evident that this particular guest appeared not to have been made aware of proper Castle etiquette.

Without so much as the courtesy a light rapping of the knuckles on his door, the countess pushed her way brazenly through it, only to launch into a breathy tirade about losing her precious aigrette, a gift of considerable worth from the queen of France, a distant cousin to the Prussian countess. 'Sir, I fear some criminal mischief has befallen it at this place,' she declared. 'Whatever shall I do?' she moaned, her violet eyes filling with faux tears.

The ever gracious Martinet listened attentively, nodding all the while as he calmly assured this agitated female visitor to his bedchamber that a thorough search for her missing gem would be instituted at once, and the culprit –

if indeed there *was* a culprit – swiftly apprehended. For by the time the lady had finished relaying her story to her host, she had made it sound as if the object had most certainly fallen into felonious hands. Unfortunately, her male listener's comforting reassurances did little to quell what appeared to be an ever-growing feminine hysteria.

Suddenly and without warning, the countess hurled herself onto the elaborately embroidered coverlet covering the Martinet's bed and raised her caged skirts high, revealing a pale and polished pudendum not unlike those the Castle barber meticulously sheared of hair each and every morning. 'Am I not beautiful?' she cried, parting her pale thighs wide to offer the Martinet an enhanced view of her intimate charms.

Such bold actions on the part of the Prussian countess proved a great shock to the erotically seasoned Martinet. However, even more of a shock was the unforeseen absence of curls upon his patrician caller's pubic mound. Such a charming fashion had always been a requirement for the Castle's female slaves, but never had the Martinet beheld its occurrence in a blue-blooded female guest. It immediately became evident the countess was highly aroused by her host's masked blue stare. The hairless lips of her sex had opened like a blossoming flower, revealing to her onlooker a swollen and floridly flushed stamen of flesh. And as the Martinet stared at this smoothly shaven spectacle of aristocratic womanhood, the countess's clitoris beckoned to him like a crooking finger, twitching fervently and growing still redder with desire.

The Martinet continued to hover within the shadowy alcove by the door, uncertain as to what course of action to take. Diplomacy was, of course, a key consideration. Being a gentleman, he did not wish to cause offence to his titled guest. Then the countess conveniently took it upon herself to relieve the vacillating figure of her host of the necessity of making a decision. Bringing a heavily ringed hand out from beneath the caged hoop of her skirts, she positioned an experienced finger upon the sensitive button between her thighs, and commenced a complicated and dizzying series of circular movements that resulted in her shapely hips roiling to and fro on the bed. So violent were these undulations of pleasure that their observer feared the lady's bottom cheeks would cause irreparable wear to the delicate and costly silk of the coverlet beneath them.

Just when the Martinet thought it prudent to intervene and put an end to what was for him an embarrassing display, he discovered his polite declarations of protest cut off by an exhilarated cry of ecstasy. The finger of the hand causing such tremendous tumult beneath the skirts of the impassioned figure upon his bed dove recklessly into the juicing slit below, swimming happily about and leaving the Martinet gaping in helpless astonishment at this blatant exhibition of female desire – a desire directed towards him. For during all the time she had been coming to the Castle, the Prussian countess had never made a secret of her ardour for her host.

As abruptly as she had engaged his attentions, the countess rose from the now rumpled coverlet upon the Martinet's bed, tidied the chaos of her skirts, and made her way with an almost absurd sense of dignity towards the bedchamber door... although not without first painting the Martinet's speechless lips with the moist and fragrant spoils of her passion.

That evening at the supper table, as the Castle guests enjoyed a summertime meal of cold soup and cured ham along with copious cups of fruity Spanish wine, this normally aloof female guest suddenly began to act in an unusually glowing and effusive manner, the missing aigrette with its glittering spray of diamonds once again safely restored to its former place of glory above her right ear. No reference would be made to the lascivious events that had transpired within the Martinet's private quarters by either of the parties involved. Nevertheless, the Martinet henceforward went to extra efforts to never again place himself in such a compromising position. It simply could not be allowed, and the experience had sorely tempted him to consider once again bringing into use his trusty walking stick, for the lady had most surely deserved punishing.

Indeed, it had been a very long time since the Martinet had indulged in such deliciously cruel play with one of his ilk. Alas, the ladies with whom he might have enjoyed such fine frolic were all married, and the criss-crossed marks he would leave upon their privileged bottoms would be too contentious to hide from a nosy spouse. Therefore, this led the master of the Castle to seek out the young women placed in his care whose bottoms were of no consequence to anyone, save perhaps to themselves. In fact, he considered it his duty to involve himself in their special training. The repeated application of the stick to their backsides proved to be excellent preparation for later, when it came time for a slave to pleasure a guest, thus conditioning an inexperienced young female's posterior into accepting whatever might be done to it. Over the years, however, the Martinet's tastes had changed and matured, evolving into a sophisticated appreciation for matters far loftier than merely painting reddish scores upon a pair of cringing buttocks with a walking stick, although the Prussian countess would undoubtedly have been a tempting means through which to get back into practice...

Still, the proprietor of the Castle had no desire to engage in what could possibly become a complicated affair. He thought it best to keep well above such mortal matters, having already experienced firsthand the foibles of love and lust. Rather, he kept his attentions turned toward the efficient running of the household, which included the efficient running of the slaves, many of whom, because of their superior birthright, required a good deal more care in their training. Slaves not of common blood were much more difficult to train, accustomed as they were to being served themselves.

The Slaves

For those in receipt of an invitation from the Martinet, and for those whose crimes necessitated an invitation in the form of a summary dispatch, the journey to the Castle was a long and tiresome one, with many borders to cross and, for some, many seas. It was also a journey fraught with hazards. In addition to the constant threat of lawless bands of highwaymen along the roads, wars were also likely to break out at any moment as monarchs sent their soldiers into battle to fight over land so their kingdoms could grow ever more rich and powerful, no matter the cost in human lives.

Unlike the Martinet's aristocratic guests, those of lesser means would be forced to make their way to the Castle in substantially less comfort and style, arriving highly dispirited and willing to do most anything for the simple comfort of a bed and the refreshment of a bath, the brown dust of the Spanish roads having filled every orifice of their weary bodies. Yet far more than dust would be encroaching upon them once they passed through the Castle's gates. Indeed, these unsuspecting travellers often wondered if it might have been preferable to accept the rat infested dankness of a prison cell than the miserable journey they had just undergone, not to mention a fate they could never even have imagined in its baseness and degradation.

To the Martinet, these young men and women of lowly birth who escaped the sadistic clutches of a jailer after an act of criminal wrongdoing or, in some cases, an act of sheer folly, always proved the most malleable in his hands; they had already been trained to serve and obey and needed merely to have their talents redirected towards less domestic tasks. But not all conscripted into sexual enslavement at the Castle hailed from common stock or situations of domestic servitude. Just as the Martinet's guests could be identified by the blueness of their blood, so too might one of his slaves. For it was the spoiled daughters and errant sons dispatched in covert haste to the Martinet by their aristocratic, scandal-fearing parents who required the most time and attention. This time and attention took the form of special training, much of which was instituted by slaves who had demonstrated their allegiance by remaining with the Martinet long after the term of their sentence had expired. After all, it was not an easy task to take someone accustomed to a life of comfort and privilege – to a life of being catered to by others – and successfully initiate him, or her, into a life of sexual servitude, however temporary. Yet if anyone could succeed in doing so, it was the Martinet.

The compelling master of the Castle took tremendous joy from the challenge of remoulding a prideful young spirit into one whose sole goal was to provide for the absolute physical pleasure of another. Of course, if anyone ever required a bit of extra convincing, for it was not unheard of for a new arrival to forget his or her place, the recalcitrant party would find him or herself trussed to a padded table in the Castle's training chamber, this restriction of movement instilling some much-needed discipline in the transgressor. When restrained in such a fashion, these men and women became subject to the whims of their fellow slaves, who were known to exercise little mercy when offered this irresistible opportunity to indulge their suppressed desire to dominate another, just as so many others had for too long dominated them.

Nevertheless, it was rarely necessary to truss up a slave as a means of punishment or coercion. On the contrary, if the company of a particular slave was desired, a guest could summon a slave into service by much simpler methods thanks to the special bodily accessory devised by the Castle's clever host. Young men and women taking on the designated garb of slaves had the delicate points of their nipples pierced and augmented by a pair of iron rings yoked together across their torsos by a slim iron chain. Therefore, any interested parties needed only to orchestrate a convincing tug upon these links to prompt the slave of choice into full and immediate compliance.

Such practical, and by many considered flattering, accoutrements were not the only form of adornment on the firm young bodies of the Martinet's slaves. No sooner had the anxious new arrivals been directed to their slave quarters, located in an isolated wing of the Castle, than they found themselves being fitted round the waist with a cinching band made of supple hide. Slightly stiffened and made richer in tone by successive tanning, these girdles served the purpose of allowing a slave's other appurtenances to be linked firmly into place. The task of fitting the bands was typically performed by the senior slaves, who could easily be identified by the fact that their pierced parts had been graduated to rings of gold rather than the more commonly worn iron. Attached to the front of the waistbands, above both hipbones, was an iron loop, and into this pair of loops had been fitted what many came to consider the most important accessory of all, and one for which the Castle had achieved its greatest fame – a slender chain. It was this particular chain that fastened to each of the tiny iron rings piercing the corresponding flaps of the clitoral hood of the female slaves and, in the instance of the males, a single ring of iron that held the loose cowl of flesh sheltering the crown of their members, the solitary iron loop above the umbilicus providing this all-important link.

For the male slaves, this unwelcome piercing of the prepuce had been intended as more a matter of practicality than aesthetics. During those infrequent occasions when not in use, or in a spent condition of dormancy, the ring prevented their members from flopping unnecessarily about and possibly causing offence to the Castle's highborn guests, the majority of whom did not find the male organ's limp state particularly appealing. It also prevented any summary usage in the event a slave wished to dispatch his services without permission to one of his own choosing. However, there were always those of hardier spirit who, despite their restraints, endeavoured again and again to loosen the hated ring of iron, unaware it had been constructed to withstand nearly every act of tampering ever attempted. Only a slave of tenure possessed the much-coveted knowledge of how to painlessly remove the ring, a temporary freedom that could be imparted at their discretion, or at the discretion of the Martinet.

In addition to this vexing ring of male confinement, a cup-like device of black silk netting had been fitted like a second skin onto the perfumed underside of the scrotum. Rather than discreetly camouflaging, what it had in its original form been meant to do, the snug sheath propelled the male slaves' continually engorged testes outward as if putting forth an offering of ripe plums. Not surprisingly, the Martinet's female guests always launched into quite a titter over this phenomenon. The more daring of the ladies would reach out with manicured fingertips, still moist and sticky with the honey of the almond-scented sweets they had just partaken of at supper, in an attempt to pluck these shiny and even sweeter fruits from their netted bowls, consequently inspiring great havoc in the pierced members battling to free themselves from their rings of iron. This would be the moment when the senior slaves took it upon themselves to intervene, thereby granting these agitated specimens a much-needed release – a release that allowed them to perform their intended function of pleasuring a guest.

Unlike their similarly garbed male counterparts, the female slaves were continuously forced to undergo a rigorous course of adjustments to their costume, the least grievous of which involved the girdles of hide at their waists. These bands would be tightened each day so the waists of the Castle's enslaved females gave the appearance of becoming increasingly smaller. And they would, in truth, eventually become so, thus rendering them a more desirable silhouette as their hips flared out in an exaggerated manner. Like the rings of iron piercing their most delicate bits of flesh, these unyielding girdles refused to be loosened as they provided the all-important structure into which all other components were secured.

With the waistbands in place, many more adjustments needed to be attended to in the normal course of a day. To most, the circumstance of their piercing was shameful enough in itself. But for these enslaved females, both high and humbly born, a lot more about shame would soon be learned when the chains attached to the iron rings piercing the once virgin hoods of their clitorises were likewise tightened, pulling each flange of tender pink flesh apart and upward, stretching them almost beyond their limits. Usually, such an enforced elongation did not hurt the recipient much, other than perhaps causing injury to her womanly pride. The Castle's female slaves quickly grew accustomed to the strange sensation of having this once neglected sensory organ pulled taut like the string on a bow as it was forced into full exposure.

An aesthete of the highest sort, the Martinet preferred these elongated and exaggerated contours in a woman. Not only did they provide an aesthetic function, they provided a practical one as well, ensuring the feminine secrets sequestered within the shy cleavage of a slave's womanhood were lustrously bared to all. And the more proper and conventional a young lady's background, the more links he ordered removed from the chains. Such refashioned contours had long been a personal preference of his. He had first been introduced to these prodigal displays of flesh in his youth by a parlour maid of great comeliness and even greater bawdiness who made a sport of raising her ruffled skirts to flaunt a most overdeveloped and ruby-red clitoris, the resilient tips of which she lewdly pulled to each side. In fact, she often bade the eager lad to indulge in a few friendly tugs upon them himself, an invitation he enthusiastically complied with. Not surprisingly, this lusty domestic would make a major impact on the Martinet, an impact that served him well as master of the Castle.

To guarantee the success of remoulding a female slave's bashful organ of pleasure into a rich plethora of sensation-rich flesh, the Castle barber was called upon regularly to offer his own brand of expertise. A highly sought after position, and one for which enquiries were made on a continual basis in the event a retirement might be forthcoming, the role the barber played in the grooming of a slave provided him with a sense of security unknown to most serving in a domestic capacity. Each morning the dwarf-like barber summoned slave after slave to his sunny workroom, his blade honed for yet another session of meticulous paring, for the Martinet had ordered every filament of hair to be shorn from umbilicus to tailbone. A conscientious worker, the barber had no desire to shirk his duties, knowing as he did that positions like his did not exist outside the Castle's walls. Besides, he genuinely enjoyed his work and could think of nothing that would have given him as much satisfaction. Therefore, he tirelessly performed his task, his blade working expertly as it skirted its way round the pierced flesh assigned to him, spilling not even a single crimson droplet of blood.

Considering the distinctive physical characteristics imposed upon them by their imprisonment, it was no wonder many of the Martinet's slaves elected to stay on at the Castle at the conclusion of their sentence rather than return to what had once been their homes. For how might one explain the presence of the peculiar phenomena now marking their bodies as clearly as if they had been branded? Those fortunate enough to have a few pieces of gold to their names might manage to pay a smithy to cut away the rings of their bondage, if the Martinet had not already granted their removal. But how to explain to a future husband or wife the marks left behind by the girdles of hide at their waists, or indeed the holes that had been bored into their most intimate parts?

Although the men were able to camouflage these shameful reminders with a reasonable amount of effectiveness, it was altogether another matter for the women. For by the time they came to be released from the iron rings that held their womanhood open to the scrutiny and amusement of both stranger and slave alike, the delicate pink wings of flesh that had been so ruthlessly perforated were stretched to such an extent, no hope remained of them ever appearing normal again. Perhaps this explained why those enslaved females who *did* choose to leave the Castle when their sentences had ended very often found themselves wedded to a man of the cloth, or a man of more modest physical tastes who would not be inclined toward tendering an exploration of their female form; the kind of man who preferred to keep matters of the flesh discreetly hidden beneath the bedclothes and for the exclusive function of furthering the family line.

And as if such physical embellishments were not enough in themselves, there was still more to be done in the process of outfitting the bodies of the Castle's slaves, which would warrant future disgrace, specifically the unique feature added to the girdle encircling their waists. This feature was added regardless of gender, and it might be said the men suffered far more than the women from its implementation, particularly upon discovering it had placed them at the mercy of the more debauched members of their sex, although many of their enslaved female peers were strongly inclined to disagree as to who amongst them had it worse. This highly specialised feature had been suggested to the Martinet by one of his most loyal and eminent of guests, a notoriously lecherous king who very early on saw the necessity for its curious inception. 'Thou will thank me in multitude for it,' the imperial fellow had assured the Martinet with a wicked grin.

Although he did not always agree with many of this Spanish monarch's political policies, the Martinet could not help but find himself nodding in happy affirmation with the royal advice being put forth. Hence a pair of straps of a more supple and slender hide than those that cinched the waists of the Castle slaves came to be fitted snugly into the deep chasm located at the terminus of a slave's back, serving to draw each blushing buttock apart and make the timid orifice therein readily available to any guest who felt inclined to make use of it. For this specific purpose, large bowls of a rich yellow fat had been placed at handy intervals all throughout the Castle compound. Or for those who preferred a more liquid lubricant, carafes containing the locally produced olive oil were provided, even outdoors in the sun drenched courtyard, since one could never be certain when or where the urge to indulge in this perverse practice might suddenly take hold. A guest could be just as inspired to indulge himself with a male slave as with a female slave, therefore these bowls and carafes were frequently and generously replenished by the household's domestic staff. Of course, there were always those guests who enjoyed the challenge of doing without. Ergo, these self-professed purists would be directed with great subtlety by the Martinet toward exactly which of the slaves they might desire to avail themselves of, since there were some whose back entrances demonstrated a far more accommodating nature than others.

Of the Martinet's many distinguished callers, there was one stately gentleman for whom this particular practice proved an overwhelming favourite, hence the motive behind the suggestion of the contraption unlocking the cleft formed by the meeting of a slave's hind cheeks. It was not at all uncommon for members of royalty to visit the Castle, and the king of Spain – who had become celebrated at court for his extremely sizable member and its seemingly fanatical penchant for the pert and shapely buttocks of young ladies – had become a regular caller. Although he too donned the anonymity of a mask, it provided little in the way of disguise. For the Spanish king was made easily identifiable not only by the distinguishing characteristics mentioned, but by a great booming voice that seemed to cause the thick stone walls of the Castle to tremble, while a good many of its enslaved inhabitants actually did tremble upon hearing the unmistakeable imperial tones.

Whenever news of this royal personage's arrival reached the Martinet's ear, he immediately ordered his domestic staff to furnish copious amounts of fat to every nook and cranny of the Castle, including even the chapel, for the king had a reputation for possessing some very wicked tendencies. Indeed, the other guests could readily identify which female slave his majesty had just indulged himself with by the severely enlarged and reddened circumference of her sphincter, which tended to remain distended for several days. However, when some of the more handsome male slaves suddenly began to appear in the same condition, gossip quickly abounded, all of which the king remained blissfully oblivious of. When one was the king of Spain, the idle chatter of the lesser nobility mattered not at all.

Like those they had been made to serve, the Castle slaves were likewise provided with masks to wear, for they too might have royal blood running through their veins and thus needed to keep their identities a secret from those who could use such damning information against them. The Martinet could not risk the possibility of a daughter or son innocently entrusted to him by a titled family being recognised; anonymity was the key to the successful running of the household, and the Martinet took his responsibilities very seriously.

Unlike those they served, a slave had no choice in the more fashionable matters of colour or style regarding their masks as they were only allowed to wear the standard slave issue black. Yet even in their uniformity, these masks were objects of beauty made of black silk taffeta and trimmed all around with fine black lace imported from a lace maker in Chantilly. Regardless of a slave's status in the household, the masks differed neither in shape nor style. The Martinet wished for there to be no mistaking who was a slave, or indeed who was *not* a slave, lest a guest filled with too much wine and lust became exceptionally unruly and endeavoured to lay claim to another guest by accident. Hence these distinctive black masks ended any potential mistakes concerning a person's position, not to mention the embarrassment that might have resulted from such mistakes… at least they should have…

Despite all the precautions, the copious consumption of potent Spanish wine every night at the supper table was known to lead to mistakes of identity the Martinet had been hoping to avoid. A besotted gentleman's vision could grow increasingly blurred, prompting the aristocratic scarlet of a mask to turn to black along the fire-lit corridors of the Castle, even as the dancing flames of the torches set into iron sconces cast a deceptively reddish glow on what should surely have been the black mask of a slave. Anyone might make such an error under the circumstances. Indeed, it was not unheard of for a marchioness or countess to suddenly find herself being flung across the stone floor, her panniers belling out behind her as the well greased member belonging to a male guest probed hotly at the unexplored furrow between her bottom cheeks, the feminine cry of 'Unhand me, you villain!' going for the most part ignored by the happy perpetrator of the deed. Although the Martinet later attempted to smooth matters over with a contritely abstemious gentleman and an embarrassed, but not altogether dissatisfied lady, he could not offer any guarantees such mistakes would not in the future occur again. For when passions were inflamed, not even the master of the Castle could possibly control the outcome.

It was incidents such as these that accounted for the Martinet's absolute refusal to listen to his senior slaves' pleas that they be issued masks of greater prestige than the standard black. They believed they had a right to be placed higher than those who had not as yet earned their standing in the slave hierarchy. Although already distinguished by the rings of polished gold piercing their nipples and genitalia, these slaves of tenure considered it a matter of pride to be even further differentiated from their lowlier peers by donning masks of colour and more elaborate trim. This was not to be, however. Hence the Martinet's fear of further situations of mistaken identity contributed significantly to the senior slaves' frustration, and the resulting severity with which they acted in their dealings with those below them.

However, masks had never been intended to cloak an unpleasing visage. On the contrary, each of the delinquent young men and women dispatched to the Martinet possessed a very pleasing face and figure, a prerequisite for those given an option to serve at the Castle for their penance. Despite the lace-trimmed presence of their masks, one could easily discern the handsomeness or beauty of a particular wearer. The lower portion of the face always remained visible to the observer. So too did the eyes – which would always be cast down in deference beneath the lozenge-shaped slits cut into the stiffened black taffeta – and the mouth, which was always available for whatever way a guest desired to make use of it. To help draw attention to this feature, the female slaves were required to rouge their lips, this rouge being charmingly extended to the hairless pair of lips between their thighs forced immodestly apart by the pierced and elongated flesh of their clitoris. The only rouge their enslaved male counterparts were required to apply was to their nipples and the oft-penetrated entrances to their fundaments, a requirement also for the females. The Martinet wanted his slaves to understand just how thoroughly enslaved they were, and for his aristocratic callers to experience not a moment's discomfiture when in the mood for a less traditional avenue of pleasure. This calculated application of the rouge served the purpose of advertising the forbidden erotic delights so readily available by the slight tug of a chain.

Naturally, there were those for whom so blatant a flaunting of the intimate physical charms of a female or male would not be required in order to inspire them toward partaking in such dark delights. These individuals belonged to a distinctly criminal element that did not wait for the Martinet to extend to them an invitation, which was just as well, considering it was most unlikely they would have received one. The only invitation they required was that of a coach travelling along the road, a coach whose lone passenger would usually be a young lady. These brazen stalkers of human prey were known to everyone as highwaymen.

As for the unsuspecting female passengers of these hijacked coaches, they might have been spared their sentences of sexual servitude to the titled and privileged, yet they could not escape from such forms of servitude altogether. Those who tried but failed to reach their destination quite often found themselves serving as slaves of another sort. For in discovering that their comely victims possessed neither jewels nor riches, these opportunistic brigands of the road appropriated the only thing of value still remaining to be appropriated – the young lady's body.

Many a noblewoman or chambermaid was unceremoniously flung onto the back of a horse only to be taken into the dusty brown Spanish hills and tampered with by many crude pairs of hands, not to mention many crude instruments of male desire. Yet even with the highwaymen's successes, there were still more than enough engaging young females who managed to arrive quite safely at the Castle, where they were subsequently groomed by the Martinet into ideal slaves.

The Keeper of the Clyster

Many swift and silent persons operated within the gloomy shadows of the Castle – the household servants who cooked the guests' suppers and cleaned the guests' quarters. Although these invisible spirits of the kitchen and bedchamber were rarely encountered in the normal course of their duties, their presences were most keenly felt. Nearly everyone knew the Castle boasted one of the finest kitchens in all of Europe, a kitchen capable of pleasing even the most finicky of aristocratic appetites. This was not surprising, considering it was the Castle's function to please any and every appetite, although the *spécialité de la maison* tended to generally be of an erotic nature.

These unseen denizens of the household also included those whose occupations lent them a special kind of prestige, such as the Castle barber. However, there was yet one more member of the domestic staff whose contribution to the Castle's success had come to be considered of equal, if not greater, importance.

To maintain the absolute highest standards of quality in his slaves, it had become necessary for the Martinet to secure a person of rather curious talents, a person who would see to it that a gentleman or lady of title received a slave who possessed all the dewy freshness of a young virgin. For as the Castle's guest list continued to grow, so too did the number of hours a slave might be required to spend in his or her function as an object of pleasure. In fact, it was not uncommon for a slave to be dispatched

35

from one guest to another with scarcely time to draw breath between interludes.

Enter the ready and willing personage known as the Keeper of the Clyster, a post more sought after than even that of the barber. The Keeper of the Clyster was one of the individuals of domestic rank whose humble presence was never spied by the aristocratic eyes of the guests; he did not make himself known to anyone except those to whom he had been employed to administer. Unlike many of his peers, who occupied similar routine positions (for even the Castle barber experienced the occasional moment of monotony when applying his well-honed blade to pudendum after pudendum) the Keeper seemed quite content in his duties; so content he would not have wished to trade places with the Martinet himself. Indeed, he had sufficient work awaiting him without taking on the added social and administrative responsibilities of his mysterious employer. A slave was likely to visit his torch-lit workroom in the garret several times within a single day, depending upon how much activity had been engaged in. Unfortunately, the long white topcoat the curious fellow wore over his street garments did not do much to inspire confidence in those placed in his care. For the salacious gleam that manifested itself in the Keeper's eyes during the administration of the clyster generally proved more shocking than the act itself, as did his equally salacious smile, which was clearly visible beneath the black, bird-like beak protruding from his mask, a protrusion that repeated itself with feeble hopefulness beneath the lower half of his water-spattered topcoat.

Despite the seemingly superfluous nature of the Keeper's duties, such purgative procedures were all too necessary, since surely an aristocratic guest did not wish to dip his greedy stick into a well still brimming with the frothy waters of the gentleman who had gone before. And there was always the odd visitor to the Castle who stubbornly adhered to the more traditional avenues of pleasure, in which case the cleansing clyster needed to be hastily dispensed to flush out the fertile seed of a gentleman before it reached the unsuspecting womb of a female slave. Indeed, the Martinet took pride in the fact that no accidents of nature had transpired in his home, although he would not be so foolish as to stake his reputation on the pedigree of the progeny of certain highborn ladies who, upon returning to their stately residences after a stay at the Castle, gave birth some nine months later. Undoubtedly, many future ladies and gentlemen of title were descended from a common household domestic, or perhaps even a royal nemesis, a situation that provided the Martinet with considerable amusement over the years. He enjoyed many a private chortle over such misfortunes of the nobility, the most egregious of which was the much heralded birth of the future king of Flanders, whose publicly pious mother had made many calls to the Castle while her husband was busy conducting court business in Bruges. A lady of generous girth, the Flemish queen had taken quite a fancy to young Frederico, one of the Martinet's most handsome and well-endowed slaves but also one of his most lowly born.

A stable hand brought forth from the overburdened womb of a gypsy whore, Frederico had been sent to the Castle as punishment for stealing the horses of his employer and then selling them afterwards at market for a considerable profit, most of which he frittered away on drink and on the charms of women procured from a local tavern. The pedigree of a slave mattered not in the least to the fleshy queen, however, especially when it came time to be presented with a slave's muscular phallus. Frederico's member rose up with a majesty that belied his common blood as it fought an impressive battle to escape from the iron ring imprisoning it. As a matter of course, a senior slave was dispatched at once to free the object of the queen's desire, it being imperative to act swiftly whenever a lesser slave had been summoned into service.

The Flemish queen made considerable use of Frederico's impressive organ during her stay, accepting it both to the fore and aft, and sometimes even while the tongue of a female slave was in the midst of administering to her fleshy folds, a treat made all the more delightful by its rarity. To the queen, the latter scenario proved the most effective, for in this way the heavyset royal could squat quite comfortably, with each opulently rounded thigh resting its formidable weight upon the cushioned seat of a pair of chairs, thereby leaving her lower half unobstructed and ready for its duel pleasuring. As Frederico proceeded to plunge the great girth of his lowborn manhood into the eagerly distending and densely haired maw between the queen's hind cheeks, his female partner in enslavement busied her well-trained tongue with the lewdly protruding pennant of flesh located within the bearded lips of the grand lady's sex. Indeed, the queen's ragged shouts of 'Dig deeper, slave, deeper!' and 'Lick harder, slave, harder!' resounded throughout the Castle, necessitating Frederico and his partner to provide an enthusiastic answering call. Granted, all this would only take place after Frederico had already finished dispensing his services to the grasping mouth of the queen's womanhood, which probably accounted for the swarthy-fleshed and sooty-eyed infant born to the ecstatic queen some three-quarters of a year later, an infant whose strikingly un-Flemish features no one dared comment upon.

Not surprisingly, the queen had expressed to her host that she wished to take the handsomely endowed Spaniard back home with her so she might continue to receive the therapeutic services he provided. Alas, her husband had grown nearly as wide and lazy as his wife, therefore it was all she could do to unearth the puny specimen of flesh dangling limply and lethargically beneath his paunchy belly and breathe into it some semblance of animation. Indeed, it went far beyond even the loftiest of queenly dreams that she would ever succeed in coaxing this once-kingly waif of manhood into paying a visit to her fundament, let alone paying a visit with the superior skill so aptly demonstrated by Frederico.

To help lay a path for her favourite slave's arrival, the queen of Flanders had concocted what she hoped would be a believable position in the royal household for Frederico, a position that should serve to quiet rumour and suspicion. Fortunately, the lady enjoyed the stimulation of a ride whenever the weather demonstrated its temperance, her choice of conveyance being an immense ebony beast of capricious temperament that the vigorous Frederico would surely be skilled in handling. Nevertheless, the acquisition of a slave was strictly against the dictates imposed by the Martinet. If he suddenly allowed his aristocratic callers to begin procuring his slaves, he would eventually discover himself with no one remaining to serve prospective guests. The loss of his slaves would have been personally devastating as well, since the Martinet did not pass his days entirely without sexual desire. Nor, for that matter, did the Flemish queen's favoured slave, who preferred to remain on indefinitely at the Castle, for that was where the Spanish horse thief had come to indulge his own special desires.

Perhaps if the Keeper of the Clyster had been retained for the purpose of administering to the Martinet's guests, there might have been one less heir to the Flemish throne. However, the Keeper was there to utilise his talents exclusively for slave business. Sadly, the advancing of age and too many years spent in the springtime of his life tending olives ripening in the unrelenting Cordoba sun, had taken their toll, leaving as his only avenues of pleasure his wizened eyes and his palsied hands. Be that as it may, the palsy had not affected the Keeper to the point where he could not manage to take good aim. When it came time to perform his function, his hands suddenly became those of a young man, as did the thoughts inside his head. Yet although he was likewise required to administer the clyster to slaves of the male variety, their muscular orifices failed to elicit from him the same reaction as those of a female.

Of course, the Keeper knew full well that his services were in great demand at the Castle, and this lent for a certain amount of complacency on his part; a complacency that allowed him substantial latitude in how he chose to approach his work. As could be expected from this daily presentation of fleshly temptation, the Keeper came to have his personal favourites, those female slaves he particularly relished administering a good cleansing to, and with whom he drew out the process so there was no question in any of their minds as to who was in control. And if a slave ever appeared in need of a reminder, the Keeper happily took it upon himself to provide a generous and oftentimes public lambasting of warm

40

soapy liquid to her fundament, thereby quelling all rebellion.

Although most who paid a reluctant call to the garret workroom silently and docilely resigned themselves to the Keeper's crude instrument, there was the occasional firebrand who took personal offence at the procedure regardless of how many times it was performed on her. It might be imagined that the loudest indignant protesters would be the new arrivals. Yet even those who had been serving for some time under the Martinet's roof would suddenly get it into their heads to flee before the clyster could reach the anxiously contracting mouths of their bottoms, only to just as suddenly find themselves being returned to the garret by one of their enslaved superiors, thus necessitating exactly the kind of clystering the Keeper enjoyed most. Secure from the blueness of their blood, these thwarted escapees had in his eyes become a tad too uppity in their ways and required an appropriate dressing down in the gloating presence of their peers.

For the Keeper, it was these rebellious slaves who made it worth leaving the warmth and feathered comfort of his bed in the early hours of the morning for the uncomfortable starkness of his workroom. Although the Martinet had never considered it necessary to make his venerable employee privy to his slaves' true and oftentimes royal identities, the Keeper had not toiled all these years at the Castle for naught. He might not have been able to determine whether the slave squatting before him in shrinking anticipation of yet another cleansing visit from his clyster was a prince or the daughter of an earl, but he did know their pampered bodies and refined mannerisms could not possibly belong to a common stableman or chambermaid. Therefore, he never once failed in his self-imposed mission to comment loudly and lewdly upon the apparent popularity of the buttocks belonging to these suspected aristocrats, his preferred opening statement 'I see that thy fundament has enjoyed a very busy day' resulting in sharp intakes of breath from the embarrassed recipients of this lewd remark. The Keeper found it extremely amusing that he might have been the subject of one of these slaves' monarchies or duchies where such untoward assertions would surely have resulted in him losing his head to the executioner's axe.

Needless to say, the recipients of these bawdy comments could have done without such forms of unwanted flattery, not to mention the act that warranted such flattery in the first place. Although an enslaved female of tenure might look upon the frequent usage of her fundament as a compliment, and thus display its rouged and distended mouth with a pride not usually seen in one who hailed from humble origins, those of lesser slave status, most of whom were highborn, would rarely share this sentiment. Therefore, the assertions made by the Keeper of the Clyster always brought about a stinging shame to these once privileged females whose well-plumbed fundaments had unwillingly become the topic of discussion.

Inspired by his masked audience of slaves, the Keeper fetched his trusty eyepiece to better view the results of his handiwork, all the while humming thoughtfully to himself as an artist might before applying paint to canvas. He would move in extra close to the object of his scrutiny, only to tender the suggestion that the slave before him might wish to take a moment to exercise the muscles of her anus so they did not grow slack from overuse. However, rather than proposing this be done in the privacy of her slave's quarters, the Keeper demanded such an undertaking be performed at once, and before the eyes of her enslaved peers. Although he was, in truth, only a servant at the Castle, when the Keeper of the Clyster issued an order, it had to be obeyed as if the Martinet himself had handed it down. Hence the female slave whose hind opening had been deemed in need of special conditioning was forced to repeatedly contract the well-stretched ring of her fundament before the fiery eyes of not only the aged Keeper, but also of nearly every male slave at the Castle. As these young men watched their unfortunate companion in slavery, their eyes glowed from behind the black taffeta of their masks with a heat that seared the rhythmically clenching mouth between her bottom cheeks. Their pierced members extended the delicate chains imprisoning them to their limits as they played enraptured audience to her humiliation. One male slave – a slave as fair-haired and fair-fleshed as the young woman he so eagerly observed – discovered himself plagued by a sense of familiarity as to the identity of this dorsally charmed female. It was a feeling of familiarity that haunted him long after the last rush of soapy liquid had been discharged from the grasping mouth of her fundament, inspiring in him desires not at all appropriate for a common slave, and likewise inspiring from his throat a groan of pleasure that attracted a sidewise glance from the one who had been the cause of it. Alas, such pleasant ruminations as to the young woman's possible noble identity did not prevent him from spraying his frothy aristocratic seed onto his muscled belly, a spraying that prompted his tongue to dart upward to the distinctive pinkish-brown birthmark on his upper lip, instinctively cloaking it from the female slave's view. Had the Keeper's wizened old member still retained its virile ability, it would undoubtedly have done the same. Instead, the Castle's trusted servant had to content himself with ribaldry and an exercise of power, a power many at the Castle endeavoured to emulate, albeit not always with success.

Annabella

In all her days at the Castle, Annabella never became accustomed to her treatment at the uncouth hands of the Keeper of the Clyster. Although this venerable member of the household's foul instrument was daily meted out to all of the slaves, she suspected he had made of her a special case. Indeed, the Keeper seemed intent upon her continued and very public humiliation, a humiliation that bore no relation to anything she had done to deserve such a degrading and uncomfortable punishment.

There were many who would cause Annabella humiliation during the time of her sentence under the Martinet. Yet not even the most wicked and depraved of deeds demanded by the most wicked and depraved of guests compared to the disgraceful performance she was made to give before the black-masked eyes of those like herself. For there was one pair of eyes in particular that caused Annabella the most shame, eyes that were so very much like her own in their pale and placid Englishness and aristocratic hauteur that they set her limbs trembling. They were eyes that watched her at every opportunity, avidly studying the repeated clenching and unclenching of her most intimate of muscles, as if the young man to whom these eyes belonged might somehow learn the secret of her true identity this way. It was a pair of eyes Annabella tried her utmost to avoid. It was all she could do to stop herself from screaming 'Do not look upon me, sir, it is not your right!' although she suspected such protestations would not have made any difference.

The beautiful and naïve daughter of an earl, Annabella had been dispatched into the Martinet's care for the sole purpose of preventing scandal from being perpetrated upon the family name, and likewise upon the earl's ruined daughter, who by her own folly had probably forfeited any chance she had to secure a propitious match for herself. She had thoughtlessly involved herself with the lusty and equally thoughtless son of a wealthy French viscount. She had been so foolishly in love as to arrange a series of trysts with the young man, and she had even gone so far as to involve in these romantic conspiracies the servants in her father's household, servants for whom gossip was an activity of considerable enjoyment and one to be indulged in as often as possible, especially when it pertained to those who paid their wages. Therefore, it was not very long before word of the affair reached the earl's disbelieving ear. Although he had always considered his daughter innocent in the ways of the world, there were simply too many details that rang true for him to dismiss the affair.

Not a member of the social class that solved such matters by taking a strap to one's daughter's backside, this anguished father turned to a confidant who had suffered similar troubles with a son. Not a hint of scandal had blackened that family's noble name or the names of the other parties involved, most of whom happened to be titled young ladies with direct ties to the throne. Certain he had made the wisest of all possible decisions for his daughter and, indeed, for himself, the earl allowed the mysterious course of arrangements to be made. Despite his being completely unaware as to the precise nature in which his feckless offspring would be punished, the earl had been assured the girl would be well looked after and, most importantly, looked after far from the intrusive eyes and ears of their society.

Having no choice but to accept her father's faltering explanation that a swift and discreet departure would be best to prevent any further damage being done, a tearful and repentant Annabella was made to cross the rough grey Channel waters, only to find herself journeying in a simple coach, noticeably absent of the family crest, to a hot, dry and inhospitable land, journeying alone and with only a modest valise to her name. She might as well have been some nameless vagabond. Gone were the grand gowns and fine headwear and glittering jewels Annabella had taken for granted since her entrance into womanhood, and gone along with them were the dutiful servants who dressed her hair and body and tended to her every whim, no matter how fanciful or capricious or how sharply expressed. From the moment the silent driver of the coach deposited her before the Castle gates, it was Annabella who became the one doing the serving. She could never have imagined the manner of servitude into which she would be placed, not even in her most wicked dreams.

Stripped of all her stately garments and aristocratic pride, the daughter of the English earl was immediately brought before a curious fellow who gallantly introduced himself as the barber. However, this would be the first and last display of gentlemanly gallantry, for the diminutive man then proceeded to make an elaborate show of stropping his much serviced blade before finally applying it to her cringing female parts. He laboured with a deliberate slowness, humming the very same cheerful tune as that of his colleague the Keeper from beneath his barber's mask, only to extend the procedure well in excess of what was actually required to remove the silken locks he found himself challenged with. Like his fellow domestic, the Keeper of the Clyster, there was nothing the fellow enjoyed more than the virginal paring of a new arrival, especially when that arrival was a comely young woman born to the nobility, for such milky-white flesh unblemished by sun or wind could only belong to society's most privileged.

Annabella's cries of protest and indignation were met with a disciplined and bemused silence as two masked and, in this innocent newcomer's opinion, shockingly attired young women held her trembling thighs open so the musically inclined barber could more easily perform his work. Her unheeded protests graduated into a series of high-pitched threats as the two attendants unceremoniously flipped their affronted charge onto her pale belly, only to just as unceremoniously wrench apart the blushing cheeks of her bottom, thereby exposing to the eyes of those present what had never been exposed to anyone, not even to what would undoubtedly have been the very interested eyes of Annabella's beloved, the viscount's son. The barber went on to complete his duties by licking a fingertip and running it along the freshly planed crevice between her buttocks, crudely probing the pinched little opening as if testing for quality, and eliciting from its owner an astonished yelp in response.

Had she realised that henceforward this most private and shameful of places would remain thus exposed, Annabella would have protested with even greater violence. For an unyielding girdle of hide was next cinched to her slender waist, its introduction being followed by a pair of straps that fitted within the freshly shaven cleft formed by the meeting of her nether mounds. As the daughter of

48

the earl soon came to discover, these strap-like devices had been designed for the sole convenience of castle guests, serving the all-important function of holding the hind cheeks aloft from each other. The bands were drawn sharply upward, having been looped around the thighs and secured into grommets cut into the front and back of the waistband. So tight were these yokes made that the wearer felt as if the orifice they had been intended to place on display would crack from the strain. Annabella cursed her father with a tongue foul enough to shock even the most lowly born members of society, as she would curse him again and again for sending her to this terrible place. She did not feel she deserved such hellish punishment for giving herself in the heat of love to the viscount's handsome son.

Needless to say, there were many more ordeals awaiting the already transgressed-upon body of the beautiful Annabella as yet another scandalously attired young female approached the padded table upon which the disgraced newcomer was being restrained. The young woman held a slender and extremely sharp spike of iron, along with four iron rings, which she wore upon her fingers for purposes of expediency. Unlike the other two attendants, this tawny-fleshed female had a manner about her that bespoke of unchallenged authority. Indeed, the few words she deigned to utter when ordering the Castle's latest arrival into another and even more shameful pose was in a mode of pronunciation not unlike that of the French viscount's son, albeit with substantially less refinement of speech and in a tone markedly absent of any tenderness. The stern creature's black hair had been pulled back from an abbreviated forehead, and then fastened at the nape of the neck with two ivory combs, a severe coiffure framing what was quite likely a pretty face, most of which remained concealed behind the same lace-bordered masks of black taffeta worn by the other slaves, and now worn by Annabella herself. Not much else of the woman was hidden from view, however.

As she came to stand before her frightened charge, placing her smoothly barbered pudendum directly at eye level with Annabella, the young woman who had the proud designation of being the Martinet's most masterful of senior slaves, revealed to the newcomer's incredulous eyes an artificially elongated and doubly pierced clitoris glowing a bright vermilion with excitement. And so the enticing fragrance of her excitement could be more fully appreciated, this slave of tenure urged her splayed and golden-ringed womanhood into Annabella's face, which flushed to the same shade of vermilion as the tumescent object being thrust so impudently towards her. An unsuspecting novice, she had no idea how many times she would be made to service with her tongue these exaggerated sinews of female flesh or the moist crevice below. Anguished tears welled up in her eyes, for never in all her life had she been the victim of such an insult.

'How dare—?' she began, only to have her attempts at a protest cut off abruptly by the split vulva belonging to the darker woman.

For those who had been sent to the Castle, it was never too early to begin the many lessons on offer. 'Lick!' ordered the Castle's spike-wielding senior slave, her manner of speaking once again bringing to Annabella's flushing ear the accent of her beloved, although *he* would *never* have tendered so crude and impolite a demand. But then he'd had other demands to make, the most improper of which had been put forth in comforting masculine tones intended to seduce an innocent young female into raising her skirts and, in Annabella's case, spreading her legs. Why this masked woman should have desired such a strange thing from her tongue was a total mystery to Annabella. With her fine aristocratic upbringing, the genteel daughter of the earl considered herself fairly worldly; she had travelled to many foreign lands and made the acquaintance of many foreign personages, including even the king of Spain himself. Granted, she understood that what might be customary in one place was not necessarily so in another, since not every society could be as civilised as the English, and it soon became evident to her that the dispatching of a female's tongue to the intimate parts of another female was an extremely popular custom in Spain.

'Lick!' came an order of still greater insistence. It roused the two slaves restraining their charge into fits of amused snickers as they watched Annabella's quivering lips being brought forward to meet another pair of quivering lips, the latter brightly adorned with rouge and rent obscenely open by two wings of pierced flesh. Despite their having once been in the newcomer's place, this in no way inspired any sympathy within the pair. If anything, they considered Annabella's plight all the more amusing, for they already knew of the special liquid treat their stern superior enjoyed bestowing upon innocent newcomers, a treat that had become hers to bestow by right of having earned her rings of gold.

Frightened that some harm might be done to her if she did not comply with the dark-haired slave's curious demands, the Castle's latest arrival forced her timid tongue to leave the safety of her mouth, trembling visibly when it met up with the humid flesh whose womanly secrets were held forcefully open to her tentative explorations. Annabella licked and licked and licked again, a box on the ear and a tweaking of the nipple serving as her inspiration.

Wishing to aid their superior, the two slaves at Annabella's sides brought their palms down hard upon each of their young charge's bottom cheeks, the stinging blows prompting the dark notch between them to open and close like a frantically blinking eye as the shapely flesh surrounding it became suffused with redness. The repeated smacks to her backside inspired Annabella's tongue to thrust deeper and deeper into the humid cleft offered her. A slave's training commenced from the moment she or he crossed the Castle's threshold, and the senior slave Annabella discovered herself at the mercy of was considered to be the household's finest trainer.

No sooner had Annabella recovered from one indignity than she was immediately subjected to another. The necessary piercing of her virgin flesh would be done swiftly and bloodlessly and with surprisingly endurable pain, thanks to the expertise of the piercer and the surprised shock of the recipient. Yet perhaps this lack of discomfort resulted from the piercer's approval of the recipient's recent oral performance, which had demonstrated itself to be fairly satisfactory for one of such apparent inexperience. Had Annabella only realised beforehand exactly how much importance was about to be placed upon the errant movements of her tongue, she would have flicked it about with even greater enthusiasm. For many a new arrival at the Castle suffered grievously in the piercing procedure because of a reluctant tongue, the image of the slender spike just as it was about to be thrust through their most tender parts too late inducing the recalcitrant newcomers to beg for mercy.

While the earl's daughter agonised tearfully over the

iron rings now dangling from her reddening nipples, the two slaves assigned to her grooming took firm hold of her clitoris, extending its resilient tips outward as far as they would reach, whereupon the cruel instrument wielded by the slave with the masterful manner was brought swiftly forth to puncture a small hole into each delicate wing of flesh. Then, before the freshly bored openings could be given an opportunity to close back up, rings matching those that had been looped through her nipples were fitted into them, and locked securely into place. As if to further thwart their aggrieved wearer, this pierced appendage of womanhood became engorged with blood, thereby insuring the rings' permanence.

Annabella hoped these heinous crimes upon her person had finally reached an end, especially when the rings of iron were linked to their respective chains so her clitoris could be drawn sharply upward, in the same fashion as the chains belonging to the three women who attended her, the very same fashion exposing the inner pinkness that heretofore the presence of hair and labial flesh had always kept modestly hidden. Yet how terribly disappointed she was to be. For even the disgraceful ministrations of the barber and the piercings executed by a senior slave proved to be of little consequence once she found herself being introduced to the indignity of the rouge applied to her orifices.

Resigning herself to her fate, the earl's daughter allowed her body to be moved hither and thither upon the padded table by the team of slaves as the fingertip of the woman who appeared to be in charge dipped into a small pot of red powder. This brightly coloured substance was first applied with painterly precision to Annabella's lips and nipples, and then extended to include her freshly shaven

53

nether lips, which displayed a charming natural plumpness the rouge served to further accentuate. Annabella nearly wept when she looked down at herself, and saw the lips of her denuded vulva smiling back up at her like the mouth of a harlot, the tongue-like object between them stretching lewdly outward in a leering greeting.

Yet perhaps the most humiliating thing of all was the administration of the red powder to the crinkled opening that served as the private gateway to her fundament. She tried several times to cover this shameful place with her hands, only to have her arms pinned firmly and painfully down at her sides by her amused attendants. 'Hold still!' the slave nearest to her barked, rubbing her own splayed pudendum against the heel of Annabella's hand. 'Thou must be properly attired to please.'

To Annabella's chagrin, she felt the barbered little mouth of her bottom beginning to twitch beneath the dark-featured woman's forbidden touch; a twitching that repeated itself with greater intensity in the painfully stretched flesh to the fore. Such an undesired phenomenon forced a loud staccato of snickers from the one provoking it, a common guttersnipe if the earl's daughter ever saw one. She could only remember having experienced this sensation beneath the roaming fingers of the viscount's son, who had made a point of tinkering with the secluded snippet of flesh in a most vexing and, to the blushing recipient, pleasing manner. But it was intolerable she should be made to experience these feelings at the hands of a lowly creature – and a female at that.

'Dost thou like?' the senior slave hissed lovingly into Annabella's ear as she massaged the rouge in leisurely circles around the anxiously contracting ring of muscle. The woman knew from experience that the fundament would be this new slave's most sought after feature, and if the girl had a modicum of sense in her haughty English head, she would learn to enjoy its frequent use as best she could, since it would rarely be at rest. 'Dost thou like?' she repeated with greater seductiveness, teasingly probing the shy opening with her brightly rouged finger, until Annabella squirmed and squealed with discomfort and, the experienced woman suspected, with reluctant pleasure.

As if reading Annabella's thoughts, the tenured slave set aside the small pot of red powder and proceeded to stimulate the newly exposed sinews of the new slave's clitoris with a rouged finger, rubbing at the silken flesh with all the impatience of the French viscount's son, and with the same cunning premeditation as well. She even went so far as to investigate the quivering pussy below, so its fragrant wetness could be lavished behind each of Annabella's ears, thereby preparing the Castle's newest slave for the important meeting that would next take place; a meeting with the Martinet himself.

The Meeting

After Annabella had been thoroughly groomed by those assigned to her, it came time for her to be brought before the Martinet for his approval. Until now, the earl's daughter had known nothing of his existence. She only knew the Castle appeared to be populated with others like herself who had been forced into donning costumes serving no other purpose than that of allowing their most intimate parts to be exhibited like so many gaudy trinkets at market. For as the earl's daughter was led through a maze of torch-lit corridors to an entirely different wing of the Castle, she found herself being met along the way with an ostentatious parade of human flesh, a parade she would shortly and unwillingly become an important part of.

Before this could happen, however, Annabella was required to pass a rigorous inspection by the Martinet, who would then relinquish her into the expert hands of a trainer so she could be prepared to fulfil the obligations of her sentence. How Annabella trembled when confronted by the handsome face behind its elegant mask of blue. It was a blue as brilliant as the southern Spanish sky, as were the attentive eyes behind it. They flickered like hot flames as their mysterious owner casually surveyed the shivering and affronted young woman who stood awaiting his judgement. A member of the ruling class, it had never been the earl's daughter's experience to be looked at in such a manner. Nor had she ever been told she must cast her eyes down in deference when in the presence of one surely no better than herself.

Upon being instructed to remove her black mask after entering the brightly lit inspection chamber, the expression of outrage on Annabella's lovely face became all the more pronounced, as did her stinging contempt for the individual who was apparently responsible for her disgraceful new condition. Yet when the proud daughter of the earl summoned up sufficient boldness to threaten the manly figure before her with retaliation by her well-positioned father, the Martinet chuckled softly, and reminded her it had been her father who had sent her to him in the first place.

Hence, as the humbled and chastised Annabella stood quivering in fear and anger before a man who could only be a villain of the lowest and most heinous sort, the Martinet stepped forward to render a closer and highly inappropriate examination of the Castle's newest slave-in-training. Placing his weight upon one velvet-clad knee, he removed an eyepiece from the pocket of his vest and, in a distinctly businesslike fashion, put it to his eye to better scrutinise the handiwork performed by the tenured slave placed in charge of this female novice. He nodded thoughtfully, apparently satisfied the piercing of the nipples and genitalia had been done properly and that the iron rings had been fitted securely into place. Nevertheless, he decided to make a modest adjustment to the pair of chains holding Annabella's clitoris aloft by removing from them two links apiece.

It was the Martinet's expert opinion that the bifurcated wings of this doubly punctured hood could have withstood a much more aggressive stretching than they had already been given. The unwelcome climax Annabella had undergone courtesy of the rubbing fingertip of the female slave with the stern demeanour had inspired her usually sentient organ to swell to a size well in excess of the norm, giving the illusion that the chains had not been drawn as tightly as they should. Usually the Martinet would have waited at least a fortnight to perform such an adjustment to virgin flesh, however, it had become apparent from the introductory probing of his well-versed fingers at the moistening slit of her womanhood that the earl's prideful offspring had already gained a fair amount of experience with encroachments of this type, therefore, he saw no reason for delay.

Despite this newcomer's acquaintance with the more traditional avenues of pleasure, the Martinet was unable to locate any evidence of similar such encroachments having been extended to the girl's other, less orthodox, orifices. Indeed, it was these orifices that interested him the most, thanks to the unique preferences of his aristocratic guests. For reasons obvious to anyone with even a cursory knowledge of biology, the master of the Castle enthusiastically encouraged a gentleman's exploitation of such parts in his female slaves, since their usage tended to offer far less trouble over the long term.

As Annabella quaked beneath the rudely searching fingers of the Martinet, he bent her forward from her girdled waist to peer with studied concentration through his eyepiece at the freshly pared and rouged mouth of her fundament, and her trembling intensified when she felt a finger forcing a gentle, but determined, entry.

'I see thy lover has not as yet partaken of this delicious treasure,' he mused academically, finding himself charmingly answered by an embarrassed clenching of the ring of muscle his finger was in the midst of penetrating. 'We must remedy this situation at once.' And with that, he instructed Annabella to pass him a bowl of fat, which had gone previously unnoticed by her on a nearby table.

Before she could reflect more fully upon the purpose to which the rich yellow content of the bowl was about to be put, Annabella felt her rear opening being slathered with the stuff, a slathering followed by something hard and unyielding pushing at the now greased entrance to her fundament. Assuming it to be yet another discourteous finger, the earl's daughter braced herself for this additional insult to her person, only to realise what she was experiencing could not possibly belong to a hand at all. For it probed deeper and deeper, indeed far deeper than even the most determined of fingers could go...

When at last Annabella cried out it was a cry of indignation rather than pain, for the object penetrating her was far too slender to have caused the distress she had been anticipating. It was more like a massaging caress, which reached the most intimate depths of her being and left her struggling for breath. Be that as it may, the Castle's newest slave gritted her teeth until her jaw ached, because she did not wish for her masked tormentor to know that his unnatural exploration of this region of her flesh had given her a strange and shameful pleasure.

Alas, such stolen and shameful pleasures proved to be very short-lived. Just as Annabella felt the massaging device being slowly withdrawn, and the heretofore unmolested walls of her fundament retracting back to normal, the process began all over again, with one grease-slathered object being replaced by another of even greater girth. Still bent forward from her uncomfortably cinched waist, she risked a surreptitious glance behind her, and watched with childlike wonder the fat-polished hand of the Martinet as it placed the offending object that had just penetrated her onto a cloth-covered table, making no move to conceal it from her view. It was almost as if he *wanted* her to see the instrument of her disgrace, and perhaps even to admire it, for his lips stretched into a knowing smile and his elegant fingers traced the object's surface with a religious reverence, eliciting from him a longing sigh and from his observer an inexplicable shiver.

From what Annabella could discern from her oblique viewpoint, the object the Martinet had just used on her appeared to be carved from a dark wood buffed smooth of any roughness. Aside from the bulbous protuberance at one end, it assumed the shape of a cylinder, a shape that brought to mind a similarly structured object, although the one of which she had firsthand knowledge had been made of flesh-and-blood and had been the source of great personal dishonour, for it had belonged to her handsome beloved, the French viscount's son.

A series of similar wooden cylinders lay neatly upon the covered tabletop, ranging in size from the slender ones her untrained fundament had just been introduced to, to ones of alarming length and width. And seeing these objects set out side by side, from the smallest to the largest, Annabella suddenly realised exactly what the Martinet had in store for her this evening.

Taking note of the young Englishwoman's mortified curiosity, he held up for her inspection the most sizable of all the wooden cylinders. With a teasing smile he invited her to encircle its impossible girth with her hands, chuckling softly when her trembling fingers endeavoured unsuccessfully to do so. Resuming possession of it, he explained in a gentle tone that she would soon be able to accommodate it, since those placed in charge of her training would be applying the devices to her on a daily basis, until her fundament had been sufficiently coerced into accepting even the most corpulent of gentlemanly members. And indeed, the king of Spain was long overdue for one of his frequent and, for those slaves who found themselves at the receiving end of his kingly specimen, fearfully anticipated visits.

'Thy fundament shall learn to desire its fleshly counterpart with the greatest enthusiasm,' he stated almost kindly, offering her tremulous right buttock an avuncular pat of the hand, the gasp of horror that answered him the sweetest music to his ears. No doubt the innocent girl had never in her life conceived of such a trespass. He smiled with contentment; such forms of edification made his days worth living.

Although he would have liked to perform this all-important inauguration himself, the Martinet's responsibilities no longer allowed him time for such pleasantries. Therefore, as the rouged and glistening sphincter before him awaited its next punishment, he sighed weightily, a grey mist of melancholy dulling the vibrant blue of his eyes. How he longed for the simpler days when he could indulge himself with such delicious initiations. There was a time when he had primed each womanly backside with a few strokes of his ivory-handled walking stick, and then tested each female newcomer's tight back passage personally before relinquishing her to his guests, for only in this way could he be assured of her readiness to enter life as a Castle slave. Of course, the Martinet still managed to occasionally perform the final act of initiation himself if a particular slave happened to capture his fancy, as did the highly prepossessing daughter of the English earl.

Hence each day after that an increasingly humbled Annabella came to be dispatched to the Castle training chamber, where she had earlier been subjected to the indignities of the piercing spike and the rouge. Now she found herself being subjected to the even further indignities brought about by the wooden presences of the training members initially introduced to her by the Martinet. How she whimpered with wounded pride as they stretched and strained the maiden passage that had been denied her handsome beloved. She felt certain in her heart that he would *never* have dared even suggest such an unlawful and perverse penetration... although this had certainly not prevented the viscount's randy son from pondering it with hopeful anticipation when alone at night in his bed, a pondering that had led to many sticky soakings of the bed linens as he envisioned the swollen purple knob of his manhood thrusting violently and deeply between Annabella's buttocks.

Unfortunately for the Castle's timid neophyte, the slaves to whom Annabella's welfare had been entrusted were nowhere near as gentle in their ministrations as the Martinet, who preferred a sensual savouring of the process to a hasty and crude dispatching of duty. The female slave who had earlier pierced and rouged and rubbed Annabella to a wet and humiliating climax displayed a streak of cruelty that made itself known with every penetration, her sharp rebuke 'Do not whine like an infant!' prompting Annabella to cringe with renewed fear. And the woman's muscular male assistant did not demonstrate any kindnesses towards her either, what with his scant application of the lubricating fat, which did little to act as a precursor in preparing her fundament for its perverse duties. Nor did his vindictive and repeated pinching of her overly stretched clitoral flesh help, something the swarthy young man seemed to enjoy doing whenever his superior's eyes were turned elsewhere. One might have thought he harboured an intense dislike of the fairer sex, although Annabella was far too innocent in the ways of the world to have understood such things as the desire of one male for another, a desire that precluded the physical charms of a female.

Perhaps these trainers recalled their own less than tender initiations at the hands of those they now replaced. Or perhaps they resented the privileged young woman whose training they had been assigned to undertake. It had been rumoured she had very close ties to the English crown, whereas they were nothing but common servants dispatched to the Martinet for crimes most would consider petty. Alas, the dark-haired chambermaid and the swarthy stable hand had no time in their lives for tenderness, especially tenderness towards one who would likely have spoken to them with a sharp tongue and ordered a birch to their humbly born backsides without a moment's hesitation. Aye, they knew the likes of Annabella very well. Therefore, it should not have been surprising that the Castle's newest female slave would be deemed ready for full servitude in less than a week's time. For having been successfully graduated to the largest of the wooden training tools, the passage of Annabella's fundament had been prized into welcoming *any* aristocratic gentleman who might desire an encroachment. As it happened, the Martinet was so pleased by her progress that he decided to initiate his blue-blooded ward into her official duties with a tool of the flesh-and-blood variety.

It was not the norm for a slave to be brought to the Martinet's private apartments. Nor was it a practice he wished to encourage. He did not think it wise for those he had enslaved to get it into their heads that they might be superior to the other slaves, and therefore deserving of special treatment. Yet every so often he came upon a slave whose charms commanded his attention, as did those of the fair-fleshed and high-spirited Annabella. How the Martinet laughed at her childish threats. She made a refreshing change from the mule-like docility of some of the lower born females who were sent to him. Although she required a firmer hand than most, it was merely so she could make a triumphant entry into her new vocation as a Castle slave. The Martinet took great pride and satisfaction in seeing the results of his work on a young woman of Annabella's class, for it was always those born to a life of privilege that provided the most challenge. And never in all his days at the Castle had he encountered such a delightful challenge as that posed by the daughter of the English earl.

Although it had been completely unnecessary for the slaves assigned to their aristocratic trainee to administer the largest of the wooden training members, the Martinet had decided the earl's headstrong offspring required an extra element of disciplining only this Herculean instrument could provide, an extra element that should surely cure her of any predisposition toward hauteur. Usually he preferred to use the menacing object as a means of coercion, its presence proving more than adequate to instil fear in the heart and in the backside of even the most recalcitrant slave-in-training. Sensing early on that the lovely Annabella might be difficult, the Martinet had wisely instructed her trainers to go the limit.

Only seven days after the silent driver of her coach abandoned her at the Castle gates, a much-humbled Annabella once again discovered herself standing before the Martinet, freshly shaved and rouged and awaiting what she believed would be her final approval. She knew nothing of the very great privilege being granted her by this nearly unprecedented summons to his private quarters; she knew only that she was as frightened and alone as she had been the first time they met. She tried valiantly to hide her anxious shivers, yet the sight of the ivory-handled walking stick lying unused in a corner of the room unsettled her careful composure. She had heard rumours amongst the slaves that its owner liked to use it upon the backsides of those slaves who did not please.

Having just undergone a rigorous week of training involving events of an unspeakable nature, the earl's daughter had at last learned not to cry out or flinch when having the most intimate parts of her body rudely tinkered with. It was a lesson she had mastered partly as a result of self-rumination, for Annabella concluded that her two masked trainers took pleasure in perpetrating these insults upon her and, therefore, she considered it a matter of pride to remain stoic as she suffered their disgraceful deeds. It was not at all unusual during the course of the day for the walls of her fundament to be rigorously exercised with one of the training devices while her tongue was being simultaneously exercised with the pierced and splayed flesh of her dark-haired female tormentor. Surely no more offence could possibly be done to her that had not already been done. Or so she thought…

As transpired during the occasion of their introductory meeting, the Martinet placed his eyepiece to his expert eye so he could embark upon a closer examination of the Castle's newest female slave. He appeared to spend an inordinate amount of time perusing the freshly stretched entryway between Annabella's nether cheeks, which the

65

straps of her costume held conveniently open to scrutiny.

'Very good,' he mused happily. 'Very good, indeed. Thy fundament has progressed nicely.'

Annabella exhaled in obvious relief. Perhaps she would be spared from being made the recipient of the evil-looking walking stick after all.

The Martinet's assessment was most accurate, for the brightly rouged mouth yawned in coquettish invitation, offering a savoury glimpse of the sumptuous pleasures waiting to be experienced at a gentleman's whim. Lightly coating several of his fingers with fat, he slipped these minimally greased digits into the cosmetically enhanced opening before him, satisfying himself with their ease of acceptance. In fact, so congenial was their welcome that he moaned with what sounded to his red-faced listener like a powerful yearning, for it had been far too long since he allowed himself to delve into the delights of the female fundament.

Such lusty activities had at one time been reserved for what proved to be a highly inappropriate and indiscreet involvement with a lady of title, an involvement that prompted the Martinet into declaring the hungering orifices of his female guests permanently off limits to his refined member. Although he had no wish to martyr himself at the throne of Eros, he could not afford to risk the important business of the Castle just for the transient pleasures of fleshly satisfaction.

The elegant Lady Langtree had entered his life at a time of great loneliness, for he had fled all he had ever known to create for himself a new life in this dry and dusty landscape. Fortunately for his aristocratic callers, the capricious politics of the day forced him into making this fateful decision to journey to southern Spain and undertake

66

possession of the family home, which had lain in near ruin since the death of his uncle, the baron.

Lady Langtree had been one of the Castle's very first guests, along with her husband, the portly and bibulous Lord Langtree, who displayed an insatiable penchant for the nubile backsides of physically favoured young males. Not surprisingly, Lord Langtree had already been the subject of one scandal, whereupon his wife decided to intervene before yet more trouble dirtied the couple's noble doorstep. Although her husband's unnatural proclivities were highly distasteful to her, her ladyship found herself imprisoned by the unbreakable bonds of matrimony. She had come into the marriage with little more than her blue blood and, if she chose to leave, she would take just as little away with her, therefore even thoughts of freedom were out of the question.

It had never been Lady Langtree's intention to participate in the goings-on at the Castle. She had merely planned to accompany her philandering spouse to ensure he confined his errant activities to the building proper and did not go seeking mischief in the neighbouring towns and villages, which he always managed to accomplish back in his native England. She suspected the locals of this primitive landscape would not be quite so forgiving, or as impressed by his title, as those at home. Ergo, while acts of the utmost licentiousness went on with impunity all around her, her ladyship could be found reading quietly and contentedly in the Castle's well stocked library, or sitting in the courtyard allowing the hot Spanish sun to tint her creamy shoulders, which was how she first came to the Martinet's attention. For in his position as host, he considered it his duty to make certain none of his guests ever became bored during their stay.

Concerned the sedate Lady Langtree had not found a slave to her liking, the Martinet proceeded to expound in blushingly explicit detail upon the various attributes of his slaves, even going so far as to discuss some of the methods involved in their training, in the event she was in possession of a sufficiently sadistic spirit to appreciate such techniques. He made a concerted effort to emphasise that the good lady should not be in any way reticent in partaking of the Castle's exotic offerings, even if those offerings came in the form of her own gender. For the Martinet had yet to meet a noblewoman willing to rebuff a libidinous encounter with one like herself, if given the opportunity. Even the most stiff-lipped of ladies discovered their careful reserves melting like butter when presented with the succulently parted sex of a female slave.

Alas, the Martinet's wholehearted endorsements of the young men and women in his care appeared to fall upon deaf ears. In actual fact, it was his own ears that did the listening as Lady Langtree chose that moment to unburden herself, since surely a gentleman in the Martinet's position could be counted upon to keep a confidence. The Martinet was surprised to learn that her ladyship entertained no erotic interests in either direction. It appeared she had grown weary of matters of the flesh, having just recently provided her husband with an heir.

A woman of considerable beauty and, as he quickly began to discover, even more considerable charm, it pained Lady Langtree's confidant to hear of such sensual apathy. Hoping he might bring a smile to her placid lips, the Martinet entrusted himself as her ladyship's personal escort, proudly displaying to her cultured eyes the many fine works of art he had amassed over the years, one of which happened to be a life-sized and flamboyantly attired portrait of himself, albeit masked in blue, painted late in the life of Thomas Gainsborough. As Lady Langtree gazed up in infatuated awe at this handsomely painted image of her mysterious host, she found herself losing her heart, which might explain how her ladyship also came to lose something of perhaps even greater value – the precious maidenhood of her fundament. Whether regrettably or not, her husband's fancy for the orifice did not extend to those of women, which meant she was possessed of a rare commodity at the Castle, a virgin bottom.

That evening, after a delicious supper of cold soup and roast pheasant accompanied by several cups of fruity wine, his lordship's wife discreetly followed the Martinet up to his private apartments where, after yet another cup of the region's potent ruby-red vintage before the crackling fire, a giddy and giggling Lady Langtree relinquished to her sympathetic host the as yet untried mouth of her fundament. To further entice him, she had brought along as insurance a special switch made from hickory she had procured from the Castle storeroom in the event the gentleman might be inclined to prime her bottom before penetrating it.

The lady's backside indeed received its priming, for the Martinet had not forgotten the unique pleasures to be gained from such an application. He took the switch to Lady Langtree's proffered buttocks with youthful enthusiasm, even if with markedly more gentleness than he might once have shown to the nether cheeks of a slave-in-training. In his mind, it was more a matter of theatre than anything else, therefore he made certain the hickory went whooshing through the air with as much noise as possible, interjecting a few enthusiastic swipes upon her ladyship's reddening rounds with his ivory-handled walking stick as well, so her experience would be all the richer, as he suspected his own would be after he had finished with her.

An excellent judge of character, the Martinet knew full well that the good lady had not come to him this evening seeking punishment, and it quickly became apparent the noblewoman had had enough. Her backside glowed as lividly as if it had been painted with the rouge as she cried, 'Take me, sir!' Lady Langtree's voice rang with passion as she bent over and parted her severely reddened hind cheeks with an uncharacteristic lewdness. 'Fill me with thy hot seed until I burst!' she elaborated eloquently.

Although the Martinet understood quite clearly what was being requested of him, he wished to prolong the lady's desire for a few moments more before giving her what she desired. With his walking stick still held in one hand, he pointed it at his guest's widely spread buttocks, teasing the opening between them with the tip by rolling it in tiny circles over the darkly crinkled rim. Lady Langtree's thighs began to tremble as he allowed the wooden tip to ever so slightly penetrate the beseeching seal, which had grown extremely wet from its neighbouring orifice and now glistened merrily in the firelight.

'Pray, do not torture me so!' pleaded Lady Langtree, her voice ragged with the gravity of her distress. 'I cannot bear it!'

The Martinet set down his walking stick. He had not employed it to torment her, but merely to make certain she was, in fact, truly ready for the act she apparently wished from him. Desiring to make the experience as pleasurable as possible for them both, he took matters very slowly, anointing the entire length of his hungering manhood with a generous amount of olive oil to better aid this unprecedented launch into her ladyship's twinkling fundament, for she shyly confessed to her inexperience when he was in the midst of positioning her for this special ingress.

Be that as it may, the Martinet could not have been more astonished when he discovered the facility with which she accepted him. One might have thought she had been spending her evenings practicing with the wooden training tools, so munificent was his welcome. With her elegant skirts raised high with little thought toward feminine modesty, Lady Langtree offered him the rosy cheeks of her hickory-heated bottom. She reached back to spread them extra wide, far wider than if they had been outfitted with the bands of hide worn by a slave. Ecstatic with joy, her ladyship welcomed with a cry of celebration each stabbing stroke of the Martinet's sturdy member, which had early on forsaken any move toward delicacy as she begged for his christening of her interior.

And so it was on each night of Lady Langtree's stay, a stay she convinced her equally ecstatic husband to extend.

Naturally, the Martinet was very pleased the couple had chosen to remain on in his home for a far longer time than usual. For what better form of flattery could there be for a host than to have a guest desire his company? Yet this time it was different; there was much more to it than that. Never in all his days had the Martinet spoken such words of love to any woman. Deeply entrenched inside her ladyship's bottom, he at last gave voice to the ultimate confession, the utterance of which resulted in an unusually generous outpouring of liquid love into her hot depths.

Alas, their inevitable parting nearly proved to be the Martinet's undoing, an undoing that would have brought the crenulated roof of the Castle crumbling down over his head had he not regained his senses in time.

On what would prove to be their last evening together, a dishevelled Lady Langtree flung herself at the Martinet's feet, clinging despairingly to his coattails to proclaim wildly, and with scant regard as to who might overhear, that she would leave her husband his lordship at once, just as she would leave behind the infant child she had recently borne him. However, the Martinet coolly shook his head. Such things simply could *not* be allowed.

'Sir, does not my fundament please thee?' Lady Langtree asked tearfully, her fingernails clawing frantically at the laces of the Martinet's elegant breeches. 'I am willing to do whatever is required to improve its quality. Indeed, I will stretch it to the width of *two* manly members, if such is thy desire. Thrash me with switches until I bleed, but *please* do not forsake me, my beloved!' For suddenly nothing mattered to her ladyship except giving herself in love and in lust to this blue-masked man whose face she had never fully seen yet which she cherished with all her being.

As events of this type generally go, Lady Langtree returned broken-hearted and defeated to England with her husband – although not before the couple's propitious escape from a band of highwaymen outside Cordoba – never to cross the Castle's threshold ever again. Notwithstanding, Lord Langtree returned to these dangerous parts many more times, and with significantly greater licentiousness now that he was minus the watchful eye of his wife. Her ladyship would stoically bear his lordship several more heirs, only to swiftly relinquish them into the care of a wet nurse. Sadly, Lady Langtree had become a ghost in her own home, a ghost with no interest in anything but the memory of several hot Spanish nights spent in the company, and in the bed, of a mysterious blue-masked man...

Shaking off the bittersweet past, the Martinet eagerly returned to the present, a present that, if the rouged and glimmering portal before him was any indication of, held tremendous promise. In many ways the fine-fleshed Annabella reminded him of his lost ladylove, although too many years of being sentenced to an unsatisfying marriage had encouraged several lines of disappointment to mar the pale perfection of Lady Langtree's face. Not so with the earl's young daughter, however. For despite her having known a broken heart, Annabella had not yet been made to experience the ultimate betrayal of a husband who preferred the backside of a boy to that of his wife. Suddenly, the Martinet felt a surge of tenderness for the young woman whose fundament he was about to initiate into what would be a steady progression of encounters with the male member. Aye, perhaps she might manage to avoid such marital misfortune as that which had befallen poor Lady Langtree... although this appeared most unlikely if her father the earl had a hand in the selection of her husband, as he surely would...

The Martinet smiled in self-deprecation, for the future matrimonial plans of a slave was not a subject that should have been of any concern to him. Returning his attention to the important business at hand, the master of the Castle removed several more links from the chains that kept the bifurcated flesh of Annabella's clitoris pulled unnaturally upward. This enforced elongation had so far progressed nicely. In fact, its progress seemed remarkable, considering the brief amount of time the delicate leaves of flesh had been pierced. Unless the Martinet was sorely remiss in his judgement, the hooded organ possessed an astounding responsiveness to its bonds he had seen only once, during the innocent days of his youth, thanks to the upraised skirts and lewdly tweaking fingers of the family's parlour maid.

'A most impressive specimen,' he commented academically to Annabella, taking a moment to stroke with an appreciative fingertip the silken lengths of flesh in question. Why, he could already envision the day when the rings would no longer be required and this lustrous pink appendage of femininity could be allowed to rise up in all its magnificence. He only hoped the earl's daughter would one day come to realise the great privilege given her and carry this distinctive badge of her womanhood with pride rather than shame, which would be a precious waste, indeed.

Annabella winced from the tremendous strain being placed upon her tender tips of flesh as the Martinet forced them to conform to his exacting standards. Like many of the other dastardly deeds that had been done to her since her arrival at the Castle, this deliberate distortion of her intimate parts was yet another puzzle that remained unsolved. Nevertheless, even this cruel stretching seemed agreeable when compared to the strain she would be made to experience as the Martinet began to install himself inside the brightly rouged mouth of her fundament. For having been too long deprived of this less travelled avenue of Epicureanism, he decided to forego slathering his manhood with the lubricious contents of either bowl or carafe, preferring instead to savour the unadulterated attributes awaiting him.

Although Annabella had been fully prepared for such an encounter courtesy of wooden devices applied to her fundament by her unrelenting trainers, she had *not* been prepared for the explosion that resulted when her passionate host climaxed hotly and deeply inside her. She groaned wretchedly as she felt herself being filled and filled until she thought she too would explode. And just when it seemed the onslaught had finally spent itself, the Martinet's pulsing member spewed forth still more of its hot offerings into her smouldering bottom, the name of his former beloved taking shape upon his lips.

As in his first delicious union with Lady Langtree's maiden orifice, the Martinet dispatched his thrusts with aggression into Annabella's newly trained passageway, his adamant manhood giving no indication of tiring. If anything, his erection gathered strength for yet another liquid bombardment, inspired by the quiet whimpers emanating from the stooped female figure before him. And when his second release came, it overflowed his overfilled receptacle, trickling down the hairless ravine between the reddened cheeks cushioning his thrusts.

Afterward, the Castle's latest initiate bowed low before the Martinet in obeisance, so she could kiss the manly object that had inspired such a tremendous tumult in her innards. 'I thank thee, sire, for the great blessings bestowed unto this undeserving servant by thee,' she uttered softly, very careful to affect the formal manner of speech required from those who served as Castle slaves. Her bare knees knocked together with fear, for she did not wish to even contemplate what might be done to her if she had not pleased him. The Martinet's ivory-handled walking stick waited patiently in a corner, seeming to suggest its willingness to be put to use upon those whom its owner deemed failures.

Alas, the sensation of Annabella's heavily rouged lips

upon the still-throbbing knob of his member so excited the Martinet that he could do naught but bend his blue-blooded slave forward for yet another delightful and, to both parties, unexpected foray into the successfully trained passage of her fundament, filling it still again with the sizzling fluids of his lust.

Perhaps what had so stirred the Martinet was the fact that he was the very first man to ever visit this special sanctum, although he would most assuredly *not* be the last. For the beautiful daughter of the English earl would become highly sought after by the Castle's discerning guests, one of whom happened to be the very same French viscount whose handsome son Annabella had been so indiscreetly, and so disastrously, in love with.

Annabella as Favoured Slave

In his almost continual quest to escape from his wife, the viscount had become one of the Martinet's most frequent callers, the number of his visits rivalling even those of the Spanish king's. Indeed, the company of such malleable young females as those that could be found at the Castle provided a refreshing change for him from the contentious clutches of the woman he had been forced to marry in order to make a match for two titled and extremely wealthy French families. As divine providence would have it, once he fulfilled his duty by propagating an heir, the viscount had no need to go near his wife again. Unfortunately, the viscountess was not the kind of wife to allow the reigns of domestic control to slip from her hands. Although she might not have required her reluctant husband in her bed, she *did* require him at her table. Therefore, many a fine Paris evening was spent by the viscount attending dull suppers, which were, in turn, attended by still duller people.

Fortunately, the divine providence that had aided him many years hence with the conception of his son would once again put in an appearance. What had begun as just another tiresome evening of overly rich food and idle dinner chatter did not terminate without at least the occasional moment of interest, one of which forever altered the uneventful life of the viscount. Accompanying the gentlemen guests to the library for a snifter of his best brandy, and a dash of masculine conversation regarding the politics of the day — most of which concerned the

77

recent doings of that truncated upstart, Bonaparte – the viscount suddenly discovered himself being taken into the confidence of a foreign gentleman of grand title and even grander girth, a gentleman whose presence in his home was not only a great honour but lent considerable prestige to the viscount's name.

After swilling down the contents of his host's crystal decanter, this prodigious member of Spanish royalty proceeded to let loose a tale of such extraordinary and fanciful proportions that the viscount would be left to conclude it must surely be the brandy speaking, or perhaps it was the exaggerated boastings of a tongue that had gone for too long without the taste of a woman upon it. Surely no such place as the Castle could exist, let alone the licentious events the viscount's brandy-imbibing companion professed took place therein. Did the fellow take him for a fool, the viscount wondered sourly? Yet as this mighty sovereign continued to fill his host's ear with his bombastic talk, it began to sound as if he genuinely knew of what he spoke. The details of the acts indulged in, and the descriptions of the participants with whom such an indulging had been done, sounded far too vivid to be the product of a liquor-befuddled imagination.

Not wishing to dismiss completely his stately guest's salivary ravings as those of a sexually depraved madman, the viscount listened with a sharpened ear lest such an institution as the Castle stood precisely where it was purported to, the Spain of the Moors not being altogether unknown to him in his travels. And indeed, it soon became apparent that while having journeyed across the dry, flat terrain of his guest's native land, the viscount had unknowingly bypassed terrain of a more moist and salient nature. All at once, a shiver of desperate longing shook him. It came to be followed by an audible groan as the gleeful monarch further commandeered his host's disbelieving ear by describing in salacious detail the pierced parts of the Castle's comely female residents, whose succulent pink womanhood was placed on full and exaggerated display for all to see, and to touch, liberally.

What had initially begun as a shiver evolved into a series of violent shudders that would prompt the straining front of the viscount's breeches to fill with hot sticky liquid when this royal raconteur went on to discuss the specially strapped device that forced a female's hind cheeks apart so a gentleman could freely partake of the brightly rouged aperture between them. 'Sir, it is open to any ingress,' the Spaniard wheezed into his host's eager ear. 'Open and *willing*.'

Nay, surely such heavenly delights could not be true? Yet despite his reservations, the viscount was not about to gamble with the apparent good fortune being handed his way by a gentleman of such imperial standing. Having all but gone onto his knees before the imposing figure of his guest to beg for a letter of introduction to the Castle's proprietor, the viscount, in less than a fortnight, found himself undertaking the hot and hazardous journey to southern Spain so he too might revel in pleasures the likes of which his confidant had regaled him with, pleasures he still doubted the existence of. But better to be dispatched on a fool's errand than to spend one more moment in the disagreeable company of his wife and her equally dull and disagreeable dinner guests.

The viscount could not have been more pleased with what awaited him at the terminus of his journey. Although he disapproved most vociferously of his son's reckless assignations with the daughter of the English earl, the viscount was not altogether immune to the lure of creamy English flesh or its deliciously rosy-pink hues, particularly when those hues happened to be located in places of a distinctively feminine nature. Perhaps it was no wonder that his foolhardy offspring should have discovered himself so powerfully smitten with the earl's daughter, if the slave girl with hair like finely spun flax was representative of the type. Granted, she never uttered a word in all the time the viscount spent in her company, such communications between slave and guest having been forbidden by the Martinet, yet the enslaved young woman's Englishness was apparent in her flesh and in her mannerisms. One might even have believed she had been born to the aristocracy, so refined was her comportment, and so gracefully did she move, even when executing an unladylike squat so a randy nobleman like himself might better penetrate the deepest and most mysterious recesses of her fundament, plugging it to the delicious hilt.

For having during his first visit discovered the possibility to do so existed, the viscount henceforward wasted no more time. Immediately upon each arrival, he sought out his most preferred of slaves, only to seek her out again and again within a single day, renewing his flagging strength with the cold soups and cured ham and blood sausage served in the castle's dining room. Oftentimes, the viscount's fingers would still be glimmering with the grease from the ragout of lamb he had just partaken of when he went to claim the slave he had come to consider his own. Had it not been for the unwanted existence of his wife, the viscount would have regaled the Martinet with sacks of gold coins so he could take back with him to Paris the docile figure of this finely fleshed slave. Had the viscount only realised the ruby-hewed jewel he daily plundered belonged to the renounced ladylove of his son, he might well have been more encouraging of the match.

Safe in his masked anonymity, the French viscount openly availed himself of Annabella's rouged charms with all the enthusiasm and frequency of one who has been told of his impending death. Even the dignified setting of the supper table did not remain sacred from the scene of an encounter as the viscount – to the titillated amusement of his dining companions – impatiently unlaced the front of his breeches so his favourite slave might happily sup. However, rather than partaking of a fine joint of beef like the gentleman she had been ordered to serve, the humbled daughter of the English earl would be made to partake of the viscount's fine joint of flesh, and all before the envious eyes of his masked peers, for he wielded his member with all the heartiness of a man many years younger than himself.

With the paunch of his aristocratic belly heavy with the best the Castle kitchen had to offer, the viscount allowed his wine-woozy head to fall back against the luxuriously padded brocade of his chair while the beautiful slave girl with glimmering flaxen hair, and the pierced leaves of a clitoris as juicy and pink as two slices of rare venison, bent low to take him into her lushly rouged mouth, the widely parted cheeks of her bottom inadvertently nuzzling the desire-flushed face of an adjacent diner. The lustful sounds of Annabella's increasingly expert sucks upon the French nobleman's upstanding manhood provided a harmonious song for the ears of her listeners, who failed to realise this slave had been instructed that she should by no means be subtle in her technique.

Obediently, afraid of the consequences if she did not do so, Annabella made quite a show of fellatio, both sipping and slurping the proffered member before swallowing it whole. The painful smacks upon her bottom, provided very early on by her stern trainer, had served as sufficient inducement for her to perform remarkably with the thick member belonging to the swarthy male assistant who appeared to have taken such a personal dislike to her. Each sharp sting of his palm against her hind cheeks sent the rigid object rushing deep into her throat, nearly gagging her. How cruelly her trainers would laugh as she sputtered and gasped, the repeated thrashings upon her backside growing ever more intense in their severity as this daughter of nobility was made to service the lowly member thrust between her lips. To be sure, Annabella did not wish to be sent back to the training chamber for further lessons, so she always gave remarkably good fellatio.

Not surprisingly, the fine oral skills of the earl's daughter did not go unnoticed by the man who had taken temporary control of her life. Having received a number of highly effusive compliments from his gentlemen guests about the young woman's ability to accept even the longest and fattest of specimens into her mouth, their host thought it sensible to summon the girl to his private quarters so he might discover for himself what so many had come to know, since even perfection could be improved upon. The Martinet generally did not care to burden himself with such mundane activities, preferring the occasional initiation of an untried fundament to all else. A self-imposed restraint cultivated over many years prevented him from participating in the orgiastic rites taking place all around him. Regarding himself as a gentleman of the utmost discipline and dignity, the Martinet had no desire to place himself on the same level as his guests, whose penchant for depravity he considered himself well above.

Notwithstanding, such carefully cultivated discipline and dignity would be swiftly put aside once the Martinet found his stiffening member being confronted by the kneeling presence of the English earl's fair-haired daughter. And what a vision she made, momentarily shaking the composure of a man even as jaded as the Martinet. Her every lip and orifice, both topmost and nether, had been generously adorned with rouge, along with the pert points of her be-ringed nipples, which had hardened even more perceptibly within the fire-lit coolness of his chambers.

'Sire, dost thou wish for thy humble slave to serve thee?' asked Annabella in a raspy, but respectful whisper, for it had been so long since she had spoken aloud that her voice seemed to have gotten lodged inside her throat. And far more than mere words would become lodged therein when a pair of dainty hands the colour of new lilies reached upward in supplication toward the heavily bobbing shaft above her, grasping it with surprising strength and with a slave's knowledge of what was expected from her.

No sooner did he pass through the rouged gateway of Annabella's lips than the Martinet found himself altering his opinion of those he had previously judged, the sensation of the swollen glans of his member massaging the silky cavern of her throat furnishing even further evidence that he had perhaps been intolerant in his thoughts. Indeed, by the time the master of the Castle felt Annabella's velvety tongue slipping down to lap at his dangerously engorged testes, he was in complete empathy with the foibles of his aristocratic guests.

With an impatience not normally seen in him, the Martinet tore loose the constricting laces of his breeches so his highborn slave could reach beneath the quivering sac of his scrotum with her industriously searching tongue. His efforts were gratefully rewarded as it flicked worshipfully across it, teasing the puckered perimeter of the opening it discovered there. The sensation all but drove the Martinet to madness, as would the return of his throbbing member to Annabella's mouth, followed by its violent spasms as he sprayed his seed deep into her frantically gulping throat. Had she not been a slave, he might have kissed the rouge-smeared lips that had helped deliver to him such sublime ecstasy. For although the Martinet had full knowledge of Annabella's pedigree, at the Castle a slave was still a slave, regardless.

Finally granting Annabella permission to stand, it now became the Martinet's turn to go to his knees as he embarked upon another adjustment to the pair of chains holding the elongated tips of her clitoris aloft. The perfume of Annabella's womanhood reached his nostrils, and he breathed it in with quiet contentment. Could it be it had grown more potent from her recent consumption of him? The possibility filled him with a curious sense of satisfaction, and with the resilient wings positioned before him in tremulous expectation of their fate, the Martinet set to work, only this time he would remove from them four links each, thereby even further exaggerating the already exaggerated contours of this bifurcated hood of flesh. Pleased with the results, he allowed himself to envision the thrilling moment when he could forego entirely the two slender chains and their accompanying rings of iron, since they would have already outlived their purpose by having successfully transformed this once demure bud of femininity into a thriving blossom of clitoral magnificence. How sad that so grand an unveiling should mark the end of a slave's time in service. Of course, there *were* those who chose to remain behind, the forbidden taste of their subjugation proving far too sweet a fruit to be so easily forsaken... as was the forbidden taste of other, even sweeter fruit...

It might have been the merest of coincidences that the Martinet presented himself with less and less frequency at the supper table on those occasions when Annabella sang and accompanied herself on the lute, only to set aside in mid-verse the pear-shaped instrument so she could pleasure the French viscount's impatient, purple-capped manhood in her mouth. The Martinet would likewise not be present to witness how his most promising female slave's forcefully parted bottom cheeks – or to be more precise, the fully exposed opening between them – captured the flustered attention of one Lady Beresford. It was her opinion that the slave's nether orifice was as garishly rouged as the mouth of a harlot, and would most assuredly demonstrate the same greedy disposition. For her ladyship, who fortuitously happened to be seated to the viscount's right, and whom all evening had remained neglected in conversation, found herself hard-pressed to ignore the sumptuous fare being presented to her inexperienced palate.

Being frequent visitors to the Castle, the arrival of Lady Beresford and her husband, his lordship, always created quite a stir. Indeed, her ladyship would not even have stepped down from the couple's elegantly equipped coach before she commenced to fan herself with her hands while complaining of the relentless Spanish heat, not to mention the dusty, bandit-infested roads they had been forced to travel over. A woman for whom the sweet blush of youth had been left well in the past, Lady Beresford discovered herself constantly plagued by the heat, even when an icy English rain was falling upon the fertile green grounds of the Beresford estate outside Aylesbury. Unfortunately, Lord Beresford – who had more libidinous matters on his mind than the climactic eccentricities of his wife – was not terribly sympathetic to her plight. Therefore, by the time the two arrived at the Castle gates, an argument of considerable amplitude would already be underway. Hearing the ruckus, the Martinet would wisely dispatch a pair of servants armed with fans made from fragrant stalks of oleander, the Moors having placed great faith in their magical efficacy, to cool the new arrivals, and perchance cool what had become an ongoing marital dispute before the other guests took notice and guessed the identities of the famously bickering Beresfords. These fan-bearing servants would even be directed to the supper table, posting themselves discreetly in the convenient vicinity of Lady Beresford. However, such efforts were all for naught as her ladyship found herself growing hotter than ever at supper when faced with the provocative presence of Annabella's buttocks.

With her husband happily occupying himself with the accommodating fundament of one of the Castle's more epicene male slaves, Lady Beresford was left free to pursue her own avenues of pleasure. For despite the enraptured interest of her masked peers, she could find very little that was either amusing or stimulating about observing the beastly transaction of her husband's stoutly mottled member thrusting repeatedly, and with the most appalling noise, into the slave boy's shapely bottom. The shapely buttocks of the female slave in the midst of orally servicing the foreign gentleman seated directly to her left began to hold somewhat greater interest for her.

Curious about what had apparently been made the object of so much masculine attention, if the exaggerated circumference of the girl's hind opening was any indication, Lady Beresford suddenly took it upon herself to insert into this brightly rouged mystery ring a very oversized parsnip that had been lying uneaten on her supper plate, grinning with wicked delight as its buttery length slid in with surprising ease. It must be noted that the parsnip was substantially fatter in girth than the fleshy specimen his lordship was presently in the midst of administering to his slave of choice – a highborn young male whose features grimaced with exaggerated pleasure beneath his black mask, for like his enslaved peers, he too had been taught well by his trainers.

Lady Beresford glanced nervously around the table to ascertain whether she had become the unwilling subject of scrutiny, and took heart that her supper companions were still eagerly engrossed in her grunting helpmate's illicit plundering of a lad young enough to have been his son, or the son of one of his aristocratic onlookers. Indeed, she could not help but smile wryly at the hypocrisy of the aristocracy, an aristocracy that all too often neglected the needs of its female members. Well, no more. Her ladyship had had enough of being a mouse in her own house, let alone in the house of another.

Hence a hotly flushed Lady Beresford set out to emulate the coarse actions of Lord Beresford's busy member by thrusting the undercooked parsnip in and out of the rouged harlot's anus, noting with distaste that both intrusive instruments possessed the same waxen appearance. Despite an initial discomfiture at this most irregular contact with another of her gender, her ladyship quickly found the activity highly entertaining and even began to giggle, especially when the nearly naked slave girl answered the clumsy plunges of the parsnip by propelling the leather-strapped cheeks of her bottom outward to meet them, thereby offering encouragement to an uncertain, albeit tenacious, female hand.

One might have assumed the enslaved young daughter of the English earl responded as she did for the primary purpose of pleasing the Castle's parsnip-wielding visitor, since her trainers had made it abundantly clear that the pleasure of a guest must always be attended to, regardless of any personal distaste on the part of a slave. However, it so happened that the anally precocious Annabella had developed a special predilection for such forms of stimuli when it came to her fundament, a predilection she had never before realised she possessed until being sent to the Castle, although this might have had more to do with the presence of the Martinet than she cared to realise. Thus Lady Beresford would be both pleased and flattered by such a plucky response from the flaxen-haired slave whom she focused her erotic attentions upon. Why, this meant that she could pleasure a woman as well, or nearly as well, as a man.

Although most of the remnants from the guests' supper plates had by now been discreetly cleared away by a swiftly moving servant, a platter of tasty sweets had been left behind, sweets made of almonds that had been fried, and then coated with rich golden honey straight from the Castle's own beehives. With her wrist tiring of its unnatural labours, Lady Beresford decided to do away with what little remained of her self-restraint. After all, why should she be deprived of indulging her fancies when her husband appeared to have no qualms about publicly indulging his? Besides which, none of her supper companions gave any indication of being the least bit interested in her. Perhaps they had already gotten it into their minds that her ladyship's activities would never be sufficiently intriguing to rival those of his lordship. Well, she would show them...

Removing one of the sticky sweets from the dessert platter, Lady Beresford placed it directly above Annabella's tailbone, allowing the glossy honey to dribble slowly and deliciously downward along the satiny roadway of flesh between the girl's forcibly cleaved bottom cheeks, where it collected invitingly at the rouged and twinkling mouth of her fundament. Her ladyship then stared defiantly at those who remained seated around the table, discerning with disappointment that matters remained much the same as before, with Lord Beresford's performance the primary focus of attention. Nevertheless, Lady Beresford – who was by this time incapable of resisting what had become the site of glory for so many – impatiently elbowed the fashionable prison of her skirts to one side so she could lean comfortably forward and partake of this glittering, honey-coated jewel with her tongue. Had she realised this very jewel had on many occasions graced the silken cushions of her settee as its fair-fleshed owner accompanied her father, the earl, to the Beresford family estate, her ladyship would have plucked out her tongue in disgrace... although his lordship would undoubtedly have looked upon the coincidental union of his wife's tongue and the fundament of the earl's charming daughter as most agreeable and something worth repeating in future, at which time he might be inclined to have a go at the girl himself.

Once Annabella finally understood just what the parsnip-wielding woman wanted from her, she ceased the wild gyrations of her buttocks, only to experience an inexplicable shiver when she felt a pair of determined thumbs plucking at the yawning rim of her fundament as they sought to further unlock the mysterious secrets within. However, what transpired next would amaze even this most presumed-upon of Castle slaves. For never had the daughter of the earl entertained the tongue of a female guest – or indeed, the tongue of *any* female – inside this most forbidden of places. Alas, it was usually her own tongue that was made to portray the aggressor by not only the Martinet's demanding guests, but by the dark-haired female slave who had ruthlessly trained her and ordered such servicing be performed in the amused presence of other slaves, including the watchful male slave with the pinkish-brown birthmark on his upper lip, as part of Annabella's course of humiliation. Granted, her sphincter had been the grudging recipient of the occasional gentleman guest whose aristocratic tongue enjoyed such a curious foray which, in her opinion, was just as unseemly as a foray of the fundament by a gentleman's member when conducted in public. And it appeared that the majority of the Martinet's guests preferred to transact their illicit business before an audience of their societal peers. Had these performers of noble rank been stripped of their masks, matters might well have been very different. Nevertheless, Annabella had all but forgotten what it was like to service a guest in private, just as she had forgotten what it was like to exert control over her own body. The Martinet had made certain her womanly attributes belonged to anyone who desired to make use of them, and the earl's daughter could think of no greater punishment.

Indeed, there seemed to be no end to this highborn slave's punishment. Having liberated herself from the restraints of her society, and desiring all those present to take note of it, Lady Beresford began to offer the cheeks of Annabella's out-thrust backside a series of enthusiastic smacks with her open hand. For now that the lady's tongue had managed to successfully lodge itself in the girl's rear passage, her hands could be free to pursue other matters, and pursue them they did, the resounding contact of flesh meeting flesh causing Annabella's bottom cheeks to flush as red as the rouge adorning the mouth of her anus, not to mention her nipples and lips, the nether pair of which could barely contain the increasingly agitated flesh of her clitoris. It looked very much as if these public torments were bringing on a wave of ecstasy to the one receiving them, an ecstasy that was in no way an act.

Taking note of the forbidden foraging and the musical smacks transpiring between his unidentified female neighbour and the lusty buttocks of his slave of choice, the French viscount's excited organ swelled to even larger proportions inside Annabella's mouth, threatening to put forth an explosion of considerable magnitude, for such transactions between two women, regardless of their social class, were highly improper, indeed. Heady with too much wine and pleasure he cheered the participants on, finding himself joined in equal measure by his table companions, whose attention had likewise become riveted to the patrician female tongue plunging in and out of the slave girl's lovely arse. 'Most excellent!' cried the viscount, his fluids abruptly bursting from him into the accommodating cavern of Annabella's throat.

'Superb!' shouted another gentleman whose member had discharged into his own hand.

'Divine!' came the strained voice of a woman overwrought with emotion as her fingers rubbed industriously between her thighs. Even Lord Beresford could not remain immune to the scene as he launched himself with one final thrust into the tight buttocks of the male slave he had bent forward over the supper table, filling him with his aristocratic seed.

Not surprisingly, it would be these very improprieties that kept the lusty viscount coming back to the Castle for more, this and the fair-fleshed female slave with hair like just-spun flax whose twin rouged mouths offered ecstasies the likes of which this French nobleman had never even dared to imagine. Hence the viscount left his native land as frequently as possible, choosing to incur the shrewish wrath of his wife rather than deprive himself a moment longer of what he knew awaited him in this dusty Spanish frontier. Not even the threat of war could deter him from seeking out the fleshly delights to be had courtesy of the Martinet, just as they would not deter others like himself whose aristocratic palates had been given an unforgettable taste of the forbidden. As for the highborn female slave whose brightly rouged charms the French viscount pursued with such proprietary regularity, Annabella would never come to know that the foreign gentleman who plundered her bottom with such wicked glee, and who now seemed to require the luxurious lodgings of her mouth as well, was none other than the father of the young man she had once loved.

Needless to say, within a matter of weeks the newly enslaved Annabella would discover her romantic dreams cruelly dashed. When she first arrived at the Castle she had entertained elaborate fantasies of a mad and daring rescue, since surely her handsome beloved would wish to secure her virtue exclusively for himself. But as the days turned to weeks and the weeks to months, this daughter of an English earl would be forced to accept the sad fact that she had been forgotten, indeed *abandoned*. Although perhaps it might have been a great deal kinder for her to be sentenced to her temporary enslavement at the Castle rather than remain at home to endure what was to come. For within days of her father's discovery of the couple's unsanctioned relationship, and his daughter's subsequent dispatch to the Martinet, the young man to whom Annabella had lovingly relinquished her precious maidenhood had gone and wed another – the beak-nosed daughter of a French marquis whose wealth made the earl a pauper in comparison. Yet he would have done so regardless of the presence of the earl's daughter, the viscount's son's betrothal to another having been well known to all in high society, or at least well known to all save for the disgraced Annabella. She had been a fool to believe his lies, but she had been young and innocent, and the centuries were littered with sad stories very much like hers.

The extraordinarily difficult adjustment to life at the Castle quickly caused this once innocent daughter of English nobility to forget her silly dreams of true love and rescue, for there was to be no rescue for poor Annabella.

Suzette

Unlike her loftier peers in enslavement, such as the beautiful daughter of the English earl whom she so delighted in tormenting, the dark-featured and very pretty Suzette had once been employed as a chambermaid in the grand château of a marquis and his family. It was not a particularly large household, including as it did the gentleman's wife and his daughter, the latter an unprepossessing young woman who was to wed the handsome son of a French viscount, and who by a fortuitous coincidence stood to receive a substantial trust on the day she took her marriage vows. Alas, such eligible young gentlemen as the viscount's son were not available to females born into a life of domestic servitude, regardless of how pleasing they were in face and figure. Nevertheless, such physical attributes might often prove to be highly useful for one who discovered herself in a compromising situation, as did the marquis's sticky-fingered chambermaid. Of course, there was always a price to be paid for one's transgressions, but for those in possession of more opportunistic natures, such a penalty could often be turned to one's advantage.

If she was anything, the marquis's former servant was opportunistic. Far away from the society she could never hope to be a part of, Suzette would at last gain parity with those she would normally be required to serve. Her life as a simple domestic in a fine residence had become as distant a memory to her as the former lives of all the other young men and women who had been sent to the Martinet for punishment by their families and employers. In the instance of this particular chambermaid, it had been the latter who sentenced her to the Castle. In the course of her duties, Suzette had had the misfortune to be caught thieving. Several articles of considerable worth had gone missing from the marquis's and the marchioness's château at Versailles, only to make their way onto the shelf of a seedy shop located at the rodent-infested terminus of a dingy Paris alleyway. Perhaps if these stolen items had not been placed on such conspicuous display by the shop's greedy proprietor, the chambermaid might have managed to continue in her post at the château until she reached an age in which she could no longer perform her duties. However, this was not to be.

When questioned by the local authorities – who suspected the merchant's procuring of such quality goods could not possibly have been managed through legitimate means – the grimy-faced Paris shopkeeper would be more than helpful in identifying Suzette as the professed owner of the stolen items. Apparently, the servant girl had frequented his place of business on numerous occasions with wares to sell; wares clearly too valuable for one of her humble station to possess, which prompted the proprietor to make his own enquiries into the matter of her identity. He had not liked the look of her one bit, although this might have had more to do with the fact that the comely young domestic had rebuffed his carnal advances several times in the course of their negotiations, the sight of the fellow's flaccid organ hanging out of his tattered breeches prompting her heart to swell with hatred.

Despite the pressing need to secure a good price, Suzette had no desire to place her own body upon the bargaining table, or in this case the bargaining *bed*. She had been strongly tempted to take a carving knife to the man as he offered her his dangling male flesh, inviting her in salacious tones to 'Come here, *mon petit fille*, and sit upon my lap.' Fortunately, the shopkeeper's ill-tempered wife took that moment to appear and quell her husband's amorous attentions before the chambermaid was required to do something in her own defence, which would most assuredly have placed her in the Bastille.

In actual fact, a rat-infested cell in the Bastille would in all probability have been her new place of domicile had it not been for the swift intervention of the influential marquis. For no sooner had the aristocratic identity of Suzette's employer become known to those who had taken her into custody than the frightened domestic discovered herself being whisked off to the château, and presented in a humbled state before the marquis who, despite the grim set of his features, did not react altogether unkindly to her plight. 'Do we not compensate you adequately enough, my dear?' he enquired, one of his caterpillar-like eyebrows slowly and purposefully curling itself into the eccentric semblance of a question mark. 'Have I not always treated you with benevolence?' he added in a magnanimously injured tone.

Flushing crimson with shame, and with rage at having been caught thieving as a result of that pig-faced shopkeeper's loose tongue, Suzette fixed her stare upon the dull leather of her shoes, unable to meet the marquis's querying gaze. The marquis was considered one of the most generous employers in all of Versailles, if not in all of France, hence the chambermaid thought it best to hold her tongue. It seemed wise not to offend the old man with any pathetic explanations for her deceitful actions, especially since she had none to give.

The marquis had been very generous with Suzette in her many years of employment at the château, even lavishing upon her little gifts of money so she might buy herself something special whenever she went to the shops. Granted, such unusual acts of generosity did not go entirely unreciprocated. Although their recipient was but a simple domestic of lowly origins, it could rightfully be claimed that the pretty young chambermaid had been very generous with her employer as well, for like his thieving servant, the marquis was not a gentleman absent of vice. It was not uncommon for him to involve himself in the occasional fiddle and diddle beneath the chambermaid's skirts as he pulled her slender form into an available cupboard. Because of the laborious nature of her work, Suzette would as a matter of comfort forego the wearing of her ruffled drawers, the coarseness and heaviness of the black cloth of her chambermaid's uniform providing adequate warmth on even the chilliest of winter days. A young woman of no means, but possessing an abundance of practicality, Suzette was not about to part with her hard-earned money, especially that which had been earned in the stifling darkness of a cupboard, in return for frivolous garments that could not be seen and whose necessity was surely open to speculation. Unfortunately, her employer chose to interpret this economic absence of undergarments as a ready invitation to partake of the feminine delights left conveniently exposed to the air, and to his gleeful tinkering.

On many a Versailles afternoon, while the marchioness unknowingly lay her powdered head upon an elegantly stitched pillow in preparation for a nap, events of a less restful nature were taking place not so far away, with

Suzette experiencing a strong masculine arm encircling her slender waist and dragging her mildly protesting form into the musty, moth-ridden blackness of a cupboard. Of course, she knew this highly determined limb belonged to the marquis, and although she could not see him clearly in the dark, Suzette could easily identify him by his smell. As a matter of personal habit, her employer liked to scent his clothing with an expensive Oriental oil that had the fragrance of myrrh, an exotic aroma that would shortly be mingling with the musky scent of the château's chambermaid's sex as the marquis's proprietary fingers forced their way between her thighs to swim in the warm pool they encountered there, diving with impunity into her innermost feminine core. On more than one occasion, Suzette's aristocratic employer had even gone so far as to boldly probe her fundament. The journey of his fingers was aided generously by the slippery wetness unearthed from her quivering womanhood, the clever marquis having had the foresight to extend his caresses to the upstanding pink peak of flesh located just above this lush female font. Perhaps it was the forbidden nature of this particular entryway that so attracted him to it, for the marquis spent an inordinate amount of time in his investigations, challenging the tightly sealed trough into accepting more and more of his fingers, until he had at last managed to introduce them all. One might have suspected this French nobleman was endeavouring to prepare his chambermaid's forbidden orifice for some unspecified future usage, as indeed he most certainly was.

All the while, Suzette never once uttered a single word of protest at these rude violations being perpetrated upon her person. For it must be noted that she had come to find the marquis's presumptuous explorations highly pleasurable, and even began to look forward to these illicit moments with anticipation, especially when her employer decided to replace his fingers with the portly shaft of his manhood, which fitted itself with unexpected ease inside her back passage. 'Your hot fundament welcomes me most amiably,' the marquis would whisper into her ear as if offering his domestic a special endearment. 'Perhaps I am not the first to have visited here?' he added teasingly, only to chuckle merrily at her heartfelt protestations to the contrary.

These frequent afternoon excursions into the cupboard, and the even more frequent excursions of the marquis's indefatigable member into the previously unplumbed depths of Suzette's bottom, prepared the chambermaid well for her future post at the Castle. In fact, events could not have been any better had they been planned beforehand, since the Martinet required his slaves, both male and female, to accept a gentleman's advances in this fashion, it being the preferred method of contact for the aristocratic classes who visited the Castle.

Therefore, it was no wonder the kindly marquis chose to intervene on his employee's behalf when informed of her crimes. Indeed, it would have broken his heart to know that Suzette had been left to grow old and haggard in a stinking prison cell, which would undoubtedly have been her tragic fate had he given the appropriate nod to the authorities, for they had seemed unusually keen to take the larcenous young chambermaid off his hands. But what were a few minor trinkets when compared to the delicious charms he had partaken of inside the velvety darkness of a cupboard? Had it not been for his sharp-eyed wife, and the château's even more sharp-eyed housekeeper, the marquis would have let the matter rest altogether. Although he might still have punished the comely offender himself with a regular course of birchings upon the cheeks of her tasty backside, for the divine abyss between them would most assuredly have been hotter than a raging fire after he finished disciplining her. However, the marchioness would have been bound to take notice of the missing items sooner or later, and better to order the swift dismissal of a sticky-fingered servant now lest the unsavoury details of the thief's assignations with her gentleman employer be brought to light in future.

Thanks to a generous gratuity paid by the marquis to the château's overly vigilant housekeeper, the issue of the stolen objects was quickly hushed up, with the marchioness spared any knowledge of such unpleasantness, especially since it had been *her* personal possessions that had found their way into the seedy Paris shop with its even seedier proprietor. The marquis had tidied up the sordid affair with as little fuss as possible, replacing what missing items he could, and then blaming the loss of the others on simple misplacement. Sadly, it was he who had lost the most in this household drama, for he came to greatly miss his pleasant afternoon trysts with the lusty chambermaid. Never in all his days had he met with so welcoming a fundament, not even when he was a swaggering young dandy whose pockets littered the streets and sidewalks of Paris with gold coins. Fortunately, he knew he could always secure passage to Spain if his longings got the better of him. The marquis routinely had reason to travel to the Spanish coast, it being most convenient for conducting matters of trade with the people of Arabia. Had it not been for his business interests in this part of the world, he might never have made the fortuitous acquaintance of the Martinet, an acquaintance that had proven highly beneficial to both parties now that the marquis's pretty domestic had been made a Castle slave. He wondered if she might still recognise the manly member responsible for introducing her spirited buttocks to such forbidden pleasures as those that had been shared in the safety and secrecy of a dark cupboard, and the thought made him smile a wicked smile, for one day he intended to find out.

Unlike her wistful employer, the château's thieving domestic would be afforded little occasion to lament the passing of the afternoon trysts that had prepared her so well for life under the inexorable rule of the Martinet. Ever since her arrival at the Castle, Suzette had lost all sense of time. The minutes of the day no longer held any meaning; morning could be afternoon, as afternoon could just as easily be evening. Everything ran together in one continual sexual stream interrupted only by meals, or by visits to the Castle barber and the Keeper of the Clyster. It was as if the former chambermaid, and the other young men and women in enslavement, had been suspended in a heavy smoke-coloured liquid whose very nature obscured both memory and volition. The Castle felt mysteriously infused with this heaviness, which seemed to affect the air itself and oftentimes made it difficult to draw a deep breath. A thick, sweetish smoke seemed to fill the rooms, a smoke that could quickly turn acrid depending upon what transpired between those who occupied them. Each time Suzette found herself being urged onto her knees and entered from behind, she could smell this smoke. It burned her nose and throat with the same poignancy as the greedy member of the anonymously masked gentleman crouching over her forcefully parted buttocks and thrusting into her burning fundament. The low animal grunting elicited by his pleasure would resound throughout the room, filling her ears until she could no longer hear the sound of her own breathing. The chambermaid sometimes imagined she had ceased breathing altogether, that all that existed of her was the brightly rouged orifice the snug bands of hide at her bottom cheeks held open, thereby exposing this once cloistered passage to anyone who desired to make use of it. And at the Castle, there would be many who desired to make use of it.

To Suzette, the odour of burning smoke, so evocative of the early days before she was rewarded with her cherished rings of gold, intensified with each plunging stroke of the greased shaft invading her uplifted backside, this particular specimen of manhood looting and plundering like the pirates who roamed the high seas off the Spanish coastline, or like the highwaymen who roamed the dusty roads leading to and from the Castle. Just when she thought the acrid smoke might choke her completely, a welling up of sensation began to make itself known in the flesh pierced cruelly by their rings of iron, which the Martinet later saw fit to replace with gold. Of course, the marquis's chambermaid immediately stifled her cry, since it was not her place to receive pleasure, but merely to be the mute provider of it.

Nevertheless, as the aristocratic gentleman filled the compliant vessel of her anus with his hot liquid ecstasy, Suzette's fingers surreptitiously flicked away the warm pearly droplets of her own pleasure that had spilled onto the insides of her thighs, the heel of her hand coming into convenient contact with the violently twitching sinews the crude pair of iron rings kept splayed, thus inducing yet another silent and mighty climax in her bound and pierced flesh. She would experience orgasms in abundance during the sentence of her punishment at the Castle, especially when it came time for *her* to mete out punishment upon those slaves of lesser status.

In her days as an *ingénue*, the château's former chambermaid learned to relish the smell of smoke. For just as it threatened to choke her, it also provided her with an intense fire of sensation – a sensation not even the marquis at his most iniquitous could have induced. The scorch marks on the thick stone walls caused by the torches burning in their iron sconces served as a constant reminder to Suzette of her new position as slave as they kept a running tally of these violations at the hands, and at the greedy members, of countless masked gentlemen of the aristocracy. For Suzette, it became a religious experience as time and time again she bowed low in supplication awaiting the aberrant blessing that was very soon to be hers. It mattered not whether this blessing was conferred by prince, earl, duke or count, for the red-rouged mouth of her bottom was open to all. It would be these smoky encounters that kept her at the Castle long past the term of her sentence, her natural affinity for them eventually attracting the Martinet's notice and earning her the Castle's prestigious rings of gold.

As for Suzette's former employer, the marquis went to great lengths to call in at the Castle as often as possible, even if his frequent journeys to Spain resulted in some unpleasantness with the marchioness, who suddenly expressed a desire to accompany her husband on his 'business travels'. This unanticipated turn of events prompted the marquis to summon his private coach well before the dear lady had risen from her bed, since the manner of business he wished to conduct would only have been hampered by the inconvenient presence of his wife. The marquis very much missed the hot-bottomed little chambermaid who had provided him with so many pleasurable afternoons in the cupboard; encounters he could never have expected to enjoy with the marchioness, let alone with the château's horse-faced housekeeper, even if the woman had been so inclined in that direction, which fortunately she was not. Like his peers, he always made certain when visiting the Castle to don his mask – a jaunty visor of crimson *moiré* taffeta trimmed with matching lace – the marquis had had made by the finest milliner in Paris, in fact the very same milliner who made all of the marchioness's extravagant hats. Such a merry coincidence provided this philandering husband with many a chortle, not to mention added considerably to the value of his mask, especially during those delicious moments when his manhood was in the midst of tasting the tight buttocks of a female slave.

Although there were very few rules at the Castle, the Martinet was absolute in his requirement that all guests wear a mask, with the same strict rule applying to all slaves, since many possessed blood as blue as those they were made to serve. Rarely did anyone argue the point; they realised it was in their best interest to guard their anonymity at all times. Surely it would not have done for a king to display himself in an untoward fashion to those who might one day seek to usurp him. Nor would it have done for a lady of the court to be seen and identified in a similarly compromising position with a slave of the same gender, thus providing the wagging tongues of the aristocracy with fodder as tasty as that enjoyed by the one accused. For the Martinet's female guests appeared to be particularly drawn toward slaves of their own sex, as was most certainly evidenced by satisfied guests like the aforementioned sweet-toothed Lady Beresford. While the marquis suffered from no such predilection as her ladyship, he still had no wish for his peers to know of his personal dealings.

Despite the seeming anonymity of Castle guests, there were certain distinctive features that could make one subject to identification. Such was the case with the marquis. Suzette could always identify her former employer, who had not altered his custom of scenting his elegant garments with myrrh. Yet perhaps this was done intentionally so the pretty chambermaid might recognise the generous patron responsible for nurturing her talents in these unsanctioned methods of pleasure and who, by his successful stint as instructor, had inadvertently saved her from the squalor of a prison cell. Yet Suzette would have known him regardless, for even after entertaining so many gentlemen of the nobility inside her bottom, she could easily distinguish the kindly marquis by the manner in which he possessed her. Each gentleman caller to the Castle exerted his own personal style when it came to such hind-wise patronage. Consequently, the château's former domestic found herself able to identify a devoted habitué by the quickness and coordination of his strokes, some gentlemen displaying a great virtuosity, whereas others merely blundered along in the act. Although Suzette would have liked to speak with her former employer, to whom she felt a debt of gratitude, the Martinet had forbidden all such communications from taking place. It was not a slave's place to speak, except amongst his or her enslaved peers, and only then out of the earshot of Castle guests.

Perhaps the marquis might also have wished to speak to his former servant, whose comely presence in the Castle he was responsible for, however, he could never be entirely certain which of the identical black masks his charming Suzette was hiding behind. Indeed, it would have proven most embarrassing for him to profess his undying adoration to one of the Castle's female slaves, only to discover she was not the thieving little minx whose backside had so enchanted his member. Although this mask business of the Martinet's was undeniably frustrating – for the marquis would not have minded observing the faces of those whose nubile bodies he used and enjoyed at his leisure – he understood the practical nature of this accessory. The anonymity of the masks also leant an even greater level of excitement to the sexual act. A gentleman might never know whose lusty buttocks he was in the midst of happily plugging; they could belong to a fine young lady of title, perhaps even a princess. Or possibly he was buggering the lovely young daughter of the financially troubled English earl who so suddenly and mysteriously disappeared from the society of her father. Now *that* would be a tasty coincidence, indeed…

From the marquis's perspective, these amusing speculations did not seem altogether without merit. There was one female slave in particular at the Castle who displayed a distinctly highborn manner. Even with her creamy white and, in his opinion, very eager bottom raised high in submissive and forcibly parted readiness, the marquis was easily able to determine that the flaxen-haired slave girl had been born into the aristocracy. Perhaps it was her apparent lack of affinity for the indecorous act demanded of her that had given away her noble birthright. For unlike her receptive and lesser-born peers in slavery, this porcelain-fleshed damsel flinched in apparent rebuff when taken, particularly when such a taking involved a spirited trouncing of the cheeks embracing this perverse vessel of pleasure. It had been this very manner of rebuff, albeit far more strongly and vociferously asserted, from the ladies of his society that had eventually driven the lusty marquis to seek out the château's chambermaid, as well as the unique hospitality of the Martinet. The marquis had no way of knowing that the seeming rebuff from the fair-fleshed slave resulted more from his erstwhile ex-employee's gratuitous assault with the wooden training tools upon her blameless backside than from any personal aversion to the act.

On those occasions when the marquis's tireless member occupied itself with the delicate fundament of the slave who did indeed happen to be the English earl's vanished daughter, his former domestic, who had since been rewarded with her rings of gold, might be found in the effete company of Sir Percival. Hailing from a society of considerable wealth, and the subsequent boredom the possession of such wealth often entails, Sir Percival was not particularly impressed by the libidinous goings-on at the Castle. Having passed the halfway point of his life, he had for the most part experienced every sexual act known to man, and then some. His method of pleasure was generally the birch, which he enjoyed having applied to his own posterior by an attractive young woman or, if one were not readily available, an attractive young man. Therefore, it should be no wonder that Sir Percival discovered himself powerfully drawn to his fellow aristocrat's former chambermaid, whose every movement bespoke of a natural ability to master and command, irresistible traits in that it was the one thing this jaded gentleman of the nobility had never been given an opportunity to experience – complete submission to the will of another.

Although not drawn toward the languid Sir Percival in exactly the same manner as he was drawn to her, Suzette did, however, undergo a peculiar sense of excitement during their turbulent encounters. For it was during these encounters when she could at last allow her innermost desire to dominate another to come bubbling to the surface. It was the same desire to which she gave unfettered reign when working in her capacity as senior slave with a female slave-in-training, only with Sir Percival it manifested to a lesser degree, the dainty and yielding form of a woman proving far more of an enticement to Suzette than that of a man. Had the marquis not sent her to the Castle, this once docile domestic might never have been granted an opportunity to realise her true nature, a nature that placed considerable emphasis upon the dispensing of punitive humiliation rather than on receiving it. It was this unique aspect of her character that had earned Suzette the Castle's much coveted tenure, thereby exempting her from having to perform the more traditional duties, such as those she had once enjoyed with her former employer. She had grown out of such simplistic occupations, leaving them to those slaves in possession of more submissive dispositions and a lower status.

Secure in the fire-lit isolation of his guest quarters, Sir Percival happily allowed the Castle's unsparing female slave to prime his cringing backside with a good birching. Unlike most of the other guests, he did not wish to place on prurient display his newly discovered predilections, which would most assuredly have made him the subject of ridicule. Although it appeared to be acceptable for the birching to be carried out by a guest upon a slave, he had yet to bear witness to a reversal of roles. Hence Sir Percival wallowed in delicious and private humiliation as the dark-featured young woman with the golden rings glinting provocatively at her nipples and clitoris stood towering over him, bringing the birch down with a sharp *thwack* against his tremulous hind cheeks. 'Pray, do not spare me!' he begged, nearly choking on his hot tears, for this senior slave possessed a most powerful right arm. Yet even this most divine of pleasures began to pale when Suzette suddenly took it upon herself to employ upon Sir Percival the very same wooden instruments used in the successful training of the earl's daughter, not to mention the other slaves whose fundaments had not as yet undergone usage. From his ecstatic cries, it appeared the gentleman had at last found his *raison d'être*. There could be no going back for Sir Percival.

Just as there could be no going back for Suzette or the other slaves who had come to the Castle. Of course, one might happen upon the occasional newcomer whose buttocks displayed a more commodious aptitude in the acceptance of their wooden encroachers. It was usually with a minimal amount of training that these slaves, who tended to be handsome young males from domestic service, the most prevalent being those who hailed from the stable still smelling of hay, found their freshly pierced and rouged persons being ushered into full servitude to entertain encroachers of the flesh-and-blood variety.

To hear his shrieks of delight, it might be believed that Sir Percival would have been far happier living life as one of these common stable hands rather than as an aristocrat who always needed to be on his guard in the presence of his peers. It was always with the greatest of enthusiasm that he raised his wan and flaccid backside to accept the highly masterful punishment meted out by Suzette, a lowly female domestic whose own arse, under normal circumstances, he would have taken a switch to just for the sheer amusement of doing so, only to afterward implant his overwrought member firmly between her birch-reddened cheeks until it had fully spent itself therein, such being his usual method of keeping his servants in order. Now instead it was the honourable Sir Percival who willingly allowed himself to be thusly implanted; implanted by an object very much like the one he would have employed upon Suzette had she been a member of his household staff in need of disciplining. Sadly, the object being wielded so mercilessly by this talented female was constructed only of wood, not of the hot manly flesh Sir Percival secretly and shamefully desired.

Perhaps it was good and right that this titled gentleman preferred the seclusion of his guest chambers to the public arena of the supper table, or the sunny courtyard with its gaily tinkling fountain, for Sir Percival's shrieks of pleasure would have proven distasteful to the cultured ears of his noble peers. With each brutal thrust of the well-greased training member into his uplifted bottom, he emitted a howl like that of a primitive jungle creature, and then beseeched his black-masked tormentor to apply it with still greater force. He would even go so far as to demand that Suzette grunt in the manner of a man as she administered the wooden tool to his desperately seeking sphincter, meanwhile demanding that she remain well out of sight behind him so he did not see her feminine parts, which would most surely have spoiled the illusion.

'Harder, sir, harder!' he croaked, obviously swept away by his fantasy. However, Sir Percival need not have concerned himself with the issuing of such instructions, as Suzette showed herself to be well up to the task, having discharged similarly cruel thrusts with the female slaves-in-training entrusted into her expert care, one of whose successful transformation had been the source of much pride, not to mention much pleasure, for the marquis's former chambermaid.

Suzette as Trainer

Suzette's special talents, such as those she demonstrated with Sir Percival, were frequently directed toward Castle newcomers, whose iron rings she too had once been required to wear before the Martinet changed them to gold. It was this training aspect of her tenure that pleased her the most. For unlike many of the others enslaved at the Castle who, because of their noble birthrights, never felt a need to be dominant, the former chambermaid had been in domestic service ever since girlhood. Therefore, she found it highly pleasurable to finally be able to exert authority over others, especially when those others were spoiled young ladies of the aristocracy.

Had it not been for an unfortunate accident of birth, Suzette might have been a fine lady herself. She could have worn beautiful garments of shiny silk taffeta, and great skirts with protrusive panniers that barely fit through doorways. She could have had finely dressed ladies and gentlemen of quality bowing to her in respect and calling her 'Your ladyship'. But instead she graduated from being a scullery maid plucking the feathers off fowl to being a chambermaid doomed to make up beds in the morning, and turn those same beds down again in the evening, leaving the afternoons to be taken up with the endless attentions of her libidinous employer, who apparently considered the paltry sum he occasionally slipped into her bodice sufficient payment for the unlimited use of all her orifices. She had been sure the door to a better life existed out there somewhere if she could only locate the key to unlock it.

Such a key finally presented itself in the most obvious of ways. In want of a few miserable pieces of porcelain or silver to trade for some coins to fill the pocket of her pinafore – a few coins that might have taken her away from a life of endless servitude, or worse yet, a life of selling her body on the streets of Paris like so many other female servants who had been tampered with by their employers – the château's chambermaid had in desperation resorted to the only avenue that seemingly remained open to her, thievery. Her wealthy employers would never even miss the modest little trinkets she managed to spirit away from the household, or so she thought.

And perhaps they never would have missed them had it not been for the château's vicious old *commère* of a housekeeper, Madame Legros, with her uppity manner and roaming hands, hands the chambermaid tried her best to stay away from. And how the spurned woman's great muzzle of a nose with its bristly black hairs reared up into the air when the larcenous Suzette was finally confronted with her crimes. The housekeeper had spoken most vociferously to the marquis about relinquishing the château's thieving servant to the *gendarmes*.

'The girl deserves the severest punishment allowable under the law,' she stated matter-of-factly, her prune-like eyes gleaming with salacious satisfaction at the image of the pretty young domestic covered head-to-toe in unspeakable filth as she crouched half-naked in a stinking prison cell with only a green-tinged crust of bread and a cup of brackish water for sustenance, steeling herself for the next violation imposed upon her by her uniformed male captors. Such a sordid image gave the housekeeper many nights of luxurious satisfaction as she rubbed herself to a climax beneath her bed sheets imagining the younger woman being held forcibly down and violated by her sadistic male captors, who finally completed the deed by discharging their briny fluids into her mouth. How Madame Legros wished she could be present to witness it all. In fact, she would have happily assisted these excellent men of the law had they granted her the privilege.

Had it not been for the timely intervention of the marquis, so horrendous an image might truly have come to fruition. For it had been he who made the private arrangements for his wayward domestic's passage to Spain, and to what would eventually be a most successful vocation under the Martinet. To encounter the marquis in society, one might wonder how so outwardly proper a gentleman could possibly have known of the existence of a place such as the Castle, let alone that his pilfering chambermaid would be welcomed there. However, the marquis was a man of many secrets, the most important of which would undoubtedly have been brought to light had he not acted to thwart its revelation.

Perhaps Suzette might have had a much easier life at the château had she relinquished herself to the housekeeper's twisted wiles. For like the lustful marquis, Madame Legros appeared most keen to get her fingers on the comely young chambermaid, a keenness that manifested itself with somewhat more subtlety than that of their male employer's. At first Suzette could never be entirely certain if the lingering touch of the housekeeper's fingertips upon her shoulder had merely been accidental or intentional, especially when those fingertips dropped still lower, brushing ever so casually across the peak of a breast, or skirting the hilly curve of a buttock, as the woman walked away from the perplexed chambermaid. During such moments, Madame Legros's equine features always remained stoically impassive save for a slight smouldering in the eyes. Nevertheless, it was only after the housekeeper began to barge without warning into Suzette's quarters when the chambermaid was alone and washing that the younger domestic's suspicions were finally confirmed.

It was as if the crafty housekeeper knew the château's pretty servant had set aside these few precious moments for her ablutions. Perhaps she had spied Suzette carrying the heavy pitcher of hot water up the back stairs to her room, which could have explained the appearance of Madame Legros at the precise moment of the chambermaid's disrobing.

As a domestic of low rank in the household, Suzette was not allowed to have a privacy latch fitted onto the door of the tiny bedchamber she shared with a scullery maid, which meant anyone could enter the room at will. Up until Madam Legros's intrusion it had not been a source of concern, since even the randy marquis had never been so bold as to venture into a servant's quarters, let alone run the foolhardy risk of being seen in an area of the château reserved solely for those of domestic status. In any event, it appeared the aristocratic gentleman much preferred the cosy confines of a dark cupboard to the more accommodating space of a bedchamber.

These unprompted visits by the château's equine-featured housekeeper continued with a steady and irksome regularity beneath the marquis's roof, with Madame Legros always justifying her arrival with some minor domestic matter she needed to discuss with the chambermaid, although why these matters could not have been discussed during the normal hours spent in the running of the household was a source of mystery to Suzette.

'I see that the marquis's personal cabinet has not been dusted today,' the housekeeper would proclaim with dramatic indignation, as the rush of cool air from the open door prompted tiny goose bumps to erupt across Suzette's bare flesh. 'The task must be undertaken at once.'

Although she dared not question the woman's undoubtedly unwholesome motives, Suzette made her displeasure and discomfiture obvious by turning away abruptly to conceal her nakedness with a discarded garment, or with the threadbare piece of cloth she had been using to wipe herself dry, leaving the housekeeper to rattle on about household duties that had apparently been neglected by the chambermaid.

Alas, Suzette's attempts to regain her modesty during these unnecessary intrusions would all come to naught, for one evening the fire that had been smouldering for too long in Madame Legros's eyes suddenly sparked into a raging conflagration, and she tore the well-worn petticoat out of the girl's fumbling hands, flinging it well out of her reach. 'I can make your work at the château a good deal easier or a good deal harder, it is entirely your choice,' the housekeeper stated hoarsely, only to supplement her words by thrusting her work-coarsened fingers between the young domestic's glistening-wet thighs, to rub with an unfeminine savagery at the shrinking nub of pink flesh hiding within the springy sorrel curls she found there. 'Do you understand?'

At first Suzette was too stunned to speak, let alone offer any form of protest. Only the marquis had ever fingered her in such a fashion, and never with so crude a touch as this. As the chambermaid's determined attacker pressed

116

relentlessly nearer to her pretty prey, Suzette smelled spirits on the woman's breath and shuddered with revulsion. She had no desire to allow this horse-faced hobgoblin of a domestic to paw her; she would take to the streets first. However, just as she moved to extricate herself from the older woman's drunken clutches, she watched in horror as Madame Legros sank to her knees, thereby replacing the rough touch of her fingers with the velvety softness of her tongue.

'Let me taste your sweet little clitty!' the housekeeper cried with inebriated desperation, her tongue lolling lewdly out toward its intended fodder. 'How I have been hungering for it...'

'Please, Madame Le—' Suzette began, and then gasped in horror. For before the young chambermaid could fully appreciate what was happening the housekeeper had already reached around to grasp her bare buttock cheeks, bringing the water-moistened mound of sorrel curls and their pinkly fleshed occupant forward to her feral mouth.

Fearing this madwoman intended some grievous harm to her person, Suzette found herself struggling in earnest. Unfortunately her valiant efforts were easily thwarted. Madame Legros held her resisting victim entrapped with fingers like iron claws, whereupon she commenced to suck elaborately, and with considerable noise, upon the chambermaid's anxiously twitching clitoral flesh, drawing the resilient hooded sinews out between her lips until the delicate appendage had nearly tripled in size.

Seemingly satisfied with her ribald handiwork, the housekeeper raised herself up from the wet floor. With a toothy smile of wicked satisfaction, Madame Legros then promptly exited the little room, leaving the door wide open so anyone passing along the corridor could observe the flustered young chambermaid contemplating the severely reddened and elongated condition of her clitoris. Never had Suzette imagined it was a condition to which she would all-too-soon become accustomed.

It so happened this would not be the only occasion when Madame Legros took it upon herself to pay an unexpected and unwanted call on the château's pretty domestic while she was alone in her quarters washing herself. Several weeks went by without further incident, with Suzette breathing many sighs of relief that the marquis's dipsomaniac of a housekeeper had apparently lost all interest in pursuing such aberrant matters, matters which in all probability had been brought on by too much drink and were therefore unlikely to be repeated. And this was precisely what the very cunning Madame Legros wished for the naïve servant girl to believe. In truth, the housekeeper was merely on the watch for a more opportune moment to present itself, so that her unusual activities with her comely subordinate would not be at risk of discovery. She would wait until the marquis and marchioness had gone off to Paris for the weekend, taking with them, as was their usual habit, several members of the household staff, including the wan mouse of a scullery maid with whom Suzette shared her lowly quarters.

Madame Legros's patience quickly paid off. On the very afternoon of their employers' departure for Paris, the crafty housekeeper once again had Suzette's naked bottom cheeks clutched within her iron grasp. The lusty woman remained blissfully indifferent to the vociferous displays of resistance that were forthcoming as she sucked harder than ever upon the pink flap of flesh in her mouth, her rough fingers rudely probing the forbidden passage explored so frequently by the more adroit fingers and

118

manhood of the marquis. As the affronted chambermaid shimmied her hips about in an effort to dislodge these intrusive female digits from her backside, she heard herself being sharply rebuked by her equine-featured superior, who reminded her that since she was so easily able to accommodate the stout member of their gentleman employer, that surely a finger or two should not bring her too much grief. '*Tch, tch*, what is this fuss? Why, your fundament has entertained far more lusty objects than these,' scolded the housekeeper, only to thrust her fingers as deeply as they could possibly go inside the chambermaid's snug trough.

Unlike the first time she had been thusly presumed upon, Suzette cried out for assistance, no longer concerned about the shameful scandal that would result should she and the housekeeper be discovered in this unnatural alliance. It mattered not that it was the chambermaid who was likely to face dismissal as a result, since it was widely known amongst those in domestic circles that a first-rate housekeeper was a good deal more difficult to engage than a common chambermaid, and therefore of substantially greater value to those who employed her.

Alas, there was no one at the château to heed Suzette's call for help. On that particular afternoon the only remaining servant was too far away, attending to more important household matters in the wine cellar, to hear these distant and desperate pleas for aid. It appeared Suzette had no alternative but to submit to these highly irregular assaults upon her private parts, for it must be noted that Madame Legros was a woman of considerable strength, not to mention considerable determination, and she was determined to conquer the chambermaid with her tongue.

It could be that the marquis's housekeeper, like her titled gentleman employer, found herself hopelessly smitten with the château's pretty young servant. The life of a domestic, especially one of such long standing, could often be lonely. However, Madame Legros's intention to force Suzette into experiencing an unwanted climax had somewhat more sinister overtones. Well past the fresh blush of youth, Madame Legros entertained no girlish fantasies about her future. Despite the courtesy title conferred upon her, she had never been married, let alone widowed, as it was so widely assumed. Nor did it appear likely she would ever lay claim to either state, her horse-like features only becoming more pronounced with age, along with the sourness of her temperament. As for any manner of alternative arrangements, it was likewise doubtful the housekeeper would enter into a sexual dalliance with the marquis, whose tastes generally ran towards females of the pert-bottomed variety who had suffered far less wear from the years. Therefore, any fleshly pleasures Madame Legros expected to get out of life would need to be procured by stealthy means. Once she managed to break the young chambermaid's will, Madame Legros had no intention of continuing these oral sessions with a girl so obviously her domestic and social inferior. Rather, it was the housekeeper's intention to initiate the pretty Suzette into performing this same oral rite upon her, and to perform it frequently and with the level of skill necessary to fan the flames of a fire that had remained dormant for far too long.

It was these unwholesome and exceedingly disturbing incidents that eventually prompted the marquis's increasingly desperate chambermaid to resort to thievery. For when Madame Legros's wily red lips at last coerced a climax of the most thunderous proportions from the slippery pink projectile she had devoted herself to suckling with such pugnacious and calculated spirit, Suzette realised her time at the château was reaching an end. And if any question as to her future remained in the chambermaid's mind, the sight of the tumescent purple banner of flesh billowing with greedy urgency beneath the housekeeper's uplifted skirts provided the final convincing, especially when its homely owner demanded prompt reciprocation. 'Lick!' Madame Legros hissed menacingly, unknowingly providing Suzette with inspiration for her future occupation at the Castle.

The horrified chambermaid's hesitation resulted in a sharp clip round the ear, followed by a strident series of threats that she would be taken out to the woodshed for a good thrashing if she did not exact the very same tumultuous results upon the housekeeper as those which she herself had experienced. 'I shall beat those pretty hind cheeks of yours until they catch fire!' the housekeeper yelled, grabbing a broomstick to offer Suzette a taste of things to come. 'Lick!' she shrieked, bringing the handle of the broomstick down upon the pale swells of Suzette's bottom again and again until the chambermaid's tongue began to do its work.

The poor servant girl found herself trapped in yet another sexual situation not of her own making, however, she vowed never to be thus trapped again. One taste of Madame Legros's clitoris proved more than sufficient for Suzette, as did the sight of the woman's darkly furred backside, which was likewise presented to the young chambermaid's unwilling but obedient tongue.

Alas, Suzette's new criminal career proved all too brief, her early efforts being met with apprehension by the authorities. What little money she had managed to hoard away from thieving, and from what she had come to consider the marquis's *gratuities*, was confiscated from her secret hiding place beneath the mattress of her bed by none other than Madame Legros herself, who somehow knew exactly where to look. Yet perhaps Suzette's humiliation at being brought before her employer to own up to her crimes might in actuality have been a blessing, for how else could she have discovered her true calling if the marquis had not seen fit to pack her off to the Castle? And once there, it quickly become apparent Suzette had a lot more in common with the imperious Madame Legros than the daily mundane chores of a household domestic.

The Martinet was pleased with the propitious arrival of this latest novitiate, dispatched to him courtesy of the good marquis, and after personally tendering a thorough inspection of her person, he happily ascertained that not only had the passage of the chambermaid's womanhood undergone moderate usage, but so had the passage of choice for his gentlemen guests, *considerable* usage, in the instance of the latter orifice. The obviously well-seasoned condition of Suzette's fundament was a most convenient find for the Martinet, who in the early days of the Castle had not yet managed to secure a sufficient number of slaves worthy of tenure, and thereby worthy of attending to the important business of training new arrivals. This frequent employment of the hind parts was generally seen in newcomers of the male variety, who either relinquished their buttocks in silent humiliation to the unnatural demands of a gentleman employer, or else in enthusiastic consent to a male peer of their own choosing.

It so happened the Martinet had encountered several

young men of both domestic background and from the aristocracy who did not require the highly specialised methods of training necessary for a successful entry into enslavement. Conversely, it had proven rare to be presented with any similar evidence of 'back door' use in a young woman, especially if that young woman claimed noble blood. The Martinet could only attribute these curious findings to the higher incidence of sexual activity undertaken by males of domestic and noble classes, as well as females in domestic service.

As for females of the nobility, they were obviously sheltered from such purported evils of the flesh, at least until marriage, at which time their well-intentioned families eagerly placed these innocents into the lecherous hands of a man oftentimes generations older than their frightened brides. For this, and innumerable other reasons, the Martinet was most grateful to have been born a man.

Like the other slaves of senior rank, Suzette had chosen to remain at the Castle well beyond the sentence of her punishment; if not for the Martinet's patronage, she would have no place to go. Despite his seeming demonstrations of benevolence toward her, the marquis had made no attempt to have his former domestic returned to service at the château, as might have been expected under the circumstances. For the marchioness had been informed by a vengeful Madame Legros of the absent young chambermaid's larcenous endeavours, although the housekeeper had stopped short of informing on the activities of the philandering marquis who, after all, paid her wages. Thus Suzette resigned herself to her fate – that she would remain a permanent resident of the Castle. Yet it was a fate she did not particularly dislike. She had grown accustomed to life under the Martinet's strict rule, finding it satisfying in a way she had never experienced while performing her chores at the château. In having left behind the tedium of domestic servitude, Suzette now hoped with the passing of each day that she would *not* be rescued, and that the marquis would forget she had ever been in his employ.

For the first time in her life, the chambermaid felt a true sense of purpose, a special calling not unlike that which might be experienced by a man of the cloth. At the Castle her work was important, as was evidenced by the pleased nods of the Martinet, who rewarded her very early on by changing her rings of iron into rings of gold. At last Suzette owned something of *real* value, something that did not have to be stolen but that had, in fact, been earned by her as a reward for her talent and skills. If the errant-tongued Madame Legros, with her lewdly uplifted skirts and her tawdry paste baubles choking her thick horse's neck, could only see her now, Suzette mused with pleasure. She was infinitely grateful to no longer have to answer to the hateful creature who had so often tyrannised her beneath the marquis's roof. Indeed, no amount of gold would have been enough for Suzette to allow the housekeeper's puckered red lips to ever again touch her private parts.

Having been promoted to Castle tenure, this once humble domestic carried herself with a new sense of pride, especially in the presence of those slaves who had not been granted such a prestigious reward. Exalting in her special status, the marquis's former chambermaid let them know at every opportunity that it had been the Martinet himself who had fitted her nipples and clitoris with these special rings – rings whose precious gold Suzette polished meticulously every morning and every evening until they gleamed even brighter than the summer sun. No doubt that fancy English tart with the perfect white skin and pedigreed family would never earn *her* rings of gold, thought Suzette, who had very early on deciphered the character of the young woman placed in her care.

And indeed, the lovely Annabella was everything the French chambermaid had always resented. Perhaps it might have been natural that a young woman born into a life of domestic service should experience so powerful an antipathy toward one born into a life of privilege and prestige, a young woman surely no better than herself except in the circumstances of money and breeding. Therefore, it was no wonder Suzette found herself going well beyond the normal call of duty when dealing with the young Englishwoman placed in her care. Although she did not know the exact details of Annabella's background – the Martinet making it a rule never to disclose any personal details about those sent to him for punishment – something about this slave-in-training brought out a lifetime of resentment in the former chambermaid, hence she made certain to act with the utmost stringency in her dealings with the earl's daughter. One barbering per day was nowhere near sufficient for this particular patrician female. Suzette would schedule a second just before supper, seeing to it with a knowledgeable fingertip that not a hint of bristle marred the blade-stinging flesh of Annabella's pale mound and hind cheeks, her scornful 'tsk tsk' another appropriate affectation learned from Madame Legros, sending the tearful girl right back into the happy hands of the barber for yet a third time in a single day. Only then did Suzette deem the earl's daughter ready to ascend to the next step.

Of course, all this extra attention on behalf of Annabella's trainer served a practical purpose as well. For once the overly indulged bellies of the Martinet's guests had been sufficiently filled with food and spirits, the slaves would all be summoned to the dining room for evening duty, appearing before these masked faces of the aristocracy freshly clystered and rouged and ready to perform any act that was bidden of them. Although she knew it was unnecessary, its girth exceeding even the grand appendage belonging to the Spanish king, Suzette chose to administer the largest of the wooden training members to Annabella's fundament before sending her downstairs, since she wished for it to be fully opened and thus ever more inviting to every gentlemen who desired to partake of it. She realised perfectly well the girl did not care for this method of trespass and, in fact, had often been heard to remark in slave circles that she disliked it intensely, which was precisely why the senior slave decided to exhibit her charge in such a blatant manner.

To ensure that her good efforts did not go unappreciated, Suzette ordered the earl's daughter to bend fully forward from the waist so her hind portions were completely bared, thereby prompting the muscular point of entry to distend slightly outward as if to kiss the probing finger. If Annabella had not bent low enough, her trainer would grasp her slender neck and urge the girl's fair head still lower to the floor, offering further encouragement by slapping her protruding cheeks until they became suffused with blood. With her subordinate at last in position, Suzette took up one of the little pots from a shelf and generously rouged the artificially enlarged socket between Annabella's well-parted nether cheeks, applying the brightest and most seductive shade of red so the yawning mouth would be all the more noticeable to the Martinet's rapacious guests, and therefore inspire the most rigorous use. Not even the mighty king himself would have been able to resist such a vainglorious specimen, even if it *was* surrounded by a young woman's flesh rather than a young man's.

Nor, for that matter, could the individual responsible for these meticulous preparations have resisted the orifice in question. To Suzette, nothing could compare to the timorous trembling of her female subordinate's lower lip when she approached with the training member, a lower lip as lusciously pink as the moist inner lips of the girl's fully exposed sex and undoubtedly as sweet, if the marquis's former chambermaid had ever been inclined to take her tongue to it.

'Why dost thou shiver so?' Suzette would tease in a falsely seductively tone, allowing her fingers to caress the pale flesh between whose twin hillocks, a rouged mouth soon to receive its oversized fodder. For each time Annabella cast her widening eyes upon the great wooden object held in Suzette's capable hands, her entire body shuddered with fear; the earl's daughter knew her punishment would be very cruel indeed. These were the moments the Martinet's senior slave had come to savour the most. Here in the Castle training chamber, Suzette could exert all the power and authority her station and gender had robbed her of, a power and authority that had lain sadly dormant within her while she had gone about making up beds at the château or slipping into dark cupboards with the ever-randy marquis and his ever-randy member.

Ergo, Suzette accepted the responsibilities of her post with grave seriousness. The fact that she so enjoyed their undertaking was an added bonus, a delightful perquisite that made all her years of domestic servitude worthwhile.

Placing her social superior onto her belly with her fine English backside raised high in apprehensive readiness, the Martinet's masterful trainer adjusted the supple straps of hide separating each perfect porcelain crescent of Annabella's bottom cheeks so they remained all the more fully and conveniently parted. Deeming her trainee ready, Suzette then pressed the flat base of the sparsely greased training device against her own sleekly shaven vulva, shivering at the sight of the enormous phallus of wood projecting out from her loins in lewd imitation of a gentleman's upstanding member. Inspired by the rosily adorned gateway quivering in fearful anticipation beneath her – for she had climbed up onto the padded training table in order to better straddle Annabella's defenceless buttocks – the former chambermaid began to stroke the tool's smoothly carved surface, her fingers slipping across its length with a calculated idleness. She felt it twitching beneath her fingertips; a twitching induced by the increasing tumescence of the exposed wings of sentient flesh the object had been strategically placed against.

Suzette's excitement at having the unprotected fundament of this beautiful daughter of the nobility right here before her, wide open and twinkling in greased expectation of what was very shortly to occur, proved almost too much for the tenured slave to endure. The former domestic shuddered in the first of many climaxes to be experienced during these preparatory pre-supper sessions, her moan of pleasure searing Annabella's disgraced ears and prompting an answering moan – a moan of pure shame. Be that as it may, not even the many long hours already spent in the rigorous conditioning of newcomers in the training chamber could have made Suzette weary of performing this rite of passage when it

128

came to the provocatively submissive form of the earl's daughter. Thus there would be many more such moans from *both* parties.

Readying herself to take aim, Suzette ground the splayed pink flesh of her clitoris against the hard base of the training instrument, feeling as the pierced flanges stretched and strained against their prestigious rings of gold. She would climax twice in this manner, only to make it thrice at the divine moment of penetration when she launched the wooden member deep into the artificially enlarged socket before her, its abrupt introduction eliciting a ragged gasp from each participant. The marquis's former chambermaid wielded the great cylinder with a masculine expertise, every stroke matching the anguished groans of her fair-fleshed victim, until Suzette felt certain a climax had been forced out of the humiliated girl beneath her. As a special reward, she would afterward allow the earl's humbled daughter to partake of her sodden female parts, which included a teasing squirt of hot piddle so that this slave-in-training did not forget her lowly place.

By the time Suzette had finished with her pleasurable plundering, the widely gaping mouth of Annabella's fundament would be in scant need of rouging, although it would receive it regardless, its delicately hued rose having effloresced into a jewel as vibrant and red as the ruby the Martinet wore upon the little finger of his right hand. Suzette smiled with self-satisfaction; how wonderfully delicious it had been to be a man for a few moments.

Alas, there were those at the Castle who did not quite share the same opinion...

Tristam

As second in line for the English throne, with only a consumptive brother awaiting the crown, young Prince Tristam could not always be counted upon to apply himself to his royal duties with the appropriate solemnity required from one of his position. Terribly concerned for the fate of the throne – for they entertained no illusions that their sickly firstborn would even live long enough to inherit it – the king and queen had been advised by their royal counsel to send their recalcitrant second son to a place of disciplining so he might be better groomed for a life of public service. For thus far, the future monarch had proven to be anything but public spirited in nature.

The handsome prince's self-centeredness and penchant toward vice had been a thorn in his parents' side since the moment of his birth, the infant Tristam having caused the queen considerable grief when he insisted upon entering the world feet first. It was a grief that worsened as the boy grew into manhood, only to flourish into parental despair when Tristam came to discover the very unique function of the fleshly object that differentiated him from those of the female persuasion.

Having left the blameless days of childhood behind, the prince continued to blunder feet first through most of his young adult life, a blundering that resulted in the compromising of several very fine young ladies of title. Consequently, many more heirs, albeit illegitimate, to the English throne were to eventually develop from such princely meanderings. Despite the sudden rash of marriages orchestrated by the noble families of these royally tampered with young ladies, the hastily procured bridegrooms were never the wiser as to the amazing fecundity of their new brides. Not surprisingly, no one ever dared mention the distinctive birthmark that manifested itself above the upper lips of so many of these couples' gurgling infants, a birthmark exclusive to those of royal blood and the family who ruled over the land and its people; such observations, if spoken aloud, might have resulted in the loss of one's head.

Nevertheless, these indiscreet matters could not be allowed to continue, for if the randy Prince Tristam persisted with his wild behaviour, he might have populated the land with enough illegitimate sons to overthrow the rightful holder of the crown. The royal family could not permit so careless a lad to ascend to the throne. A radical course of action was called for.

In the beginning Tristam showed himself to be extremely well suited for life at the Castle. In fact, so well suited did he seem to be that, had the good king and queen understood the precise circumstances of their son's penance, they would likely have elected to place him into the dangers of military service instead. And considering some of the gossip that had begun to flourish in court circles, such a pugnacious form of punishment would have been far preferable to the profligate method of punishment offered by the Martinet. For the black slave mask worn by the prince did not quite manage to conceal the telltale mark of his birth – a tiny dot of pink-hued brown appearing just above his fully fleshed upper lip, a dot that would become the subject of much hearty speculation by his fellow countrymen and women, who were already familiar with this distinctive royal insignia.

The ladies in particular mused merrily upon its significance, although it appeared extremely doubtful the Martinet's generously endowed male slave could possibly have borne the slightest relationship to the future king of England. Yet perhaps these flights of feminine fancy were what had made the young man all the more desirable in their eyes. Even before Prince Tristam had completed his traineeship, he had already distinguished himself as the most popular male slave in the Castle, a popularity further heightened by the length and appealing shape of his manhood, which arced gracefully upward when roused, and subsequently released from its confining ring of iron.

For who could lay the blame at young Tristam's feet for the sweet notes being plucked from a lute having so profound an effect upon a fine lady's sensibilities? A lady who had once never so much as even considered accepting a man into her mouth, let alone into the mouth of her bottom? Yet each lady had been as willing and eager to part with her sterling virtue as the recently enslaved English royal had been as willing and eager to take it. To think that Tristam might be servicing the mothers of the very same young ladies he had earlier treated with such cavalier disregard would have proven a most ironic twist in his punishment, indeed.

Despite the many gentlemen callers to the Castle, a number of the fairer sex were of a liberal enough mind to accompany their libidinous husbands, and even to enthusiastically partake of the many pleasures on offer, which did not always come in masculine form. Such circumstances greatly suited the carnally inclined young prince. Like those who sought out the erotic sanctity provided by the Martinet, Tristam enjoyed being granted the rare opportunity to observe a lusty exchange between two women, especially when one of the participants happened to be a certain fair-fleshed, flaxen-haired slave girl he had very much begun to fancy, and who he vowed to possess in the most forbidden of fashions before his sentence had reached an end. Of course, by that time Tristam hoped to have ascertained her true identity so matters might be allowed to continue after they had both returned to their normal lives.

During the early days of his servitude, Tristam would be called upon to spend the majority of his time with the Martinet's titled lady guests. Although most young men of his years would have shunned the mature company of these distinguished women, the Prince discovered that they provided a most refreshing change from the feathery frivolity of his former female paramours, who seemed only to have the latest French fashion on their minds, or worse yet the acquisition of a titled husband. He minded not in the least to exercise his ready member within the delightfully seasoned passages of their womanhoods, for judging from these ladies' appreciative grunts and groans, they had not experienced such divine pleasures since well before the births of their children. It was a sadly known fact that after a woman had produced the desired number of male heirs, her husband no longer required her fleshly services. Like his mysterious patron the Martinet, Tristam considered himself highly fortunate to have been born male... although he would soon have cause for lament during those occasions when a certain imperial personage paid a visit to the Castle.

Had the king and queen suspected for a moment the discipline they demanded for their unruly son consisted of the partaking of fleshly pleasures day and night – every

133

hour of the day and night – they would have dispatched a trusted deputy to bring him home at once. Yet Tristam's sentence at the Castle did not pass without a few well-earned lessons – lessons designed to humble even the most prideful and vain of newcomers. A handsomely formed young man, the heir to the English throne eventually came to the libidinous attention of the king of Spain, a situation that caused the prince considerable chagrin, since his interests had always lain exclusively with the shapely and fragrant figures of his lusty female counterparts. Now instead this slave of royal blood found himself becoming the favoured pet of the Spanish king, who had suddenly taken to increasing his visits to the Castle even to the detriment of urgent court business in Madrid.

Alas, there appeared to be little Tristam could do to thwart the heavyset monarch's determined advances. Having spent his salad days running with the hounds, the prince had developed an athletic physique that was made all the more amplified by his abbreviated slave's costuming, resulting in his well-formed buttocks being further flattered by the supple straps of hide keeping them apart, thereby placing their innermost secrets on flamboyantly rouged display. As one might have predicted, so seductive a vista had proved extraordinarily difficult for the imperial Spanish pederast to resist. Yet why *should* he have resisted? It was for precisely these kinds of forbidden delights that the king had come to the Castle in the first place, so he did *not* resist.

How poor Tristam would tremble when word fell upon his cringing ear that a certain golden coach carrying a certain prodigious passenger had just drawn up to the Castle gates. In only a matter of moments he was summoned by a senior slave, only to find himself being brought before the Martinet's honoured sovereign caller, freshly clystered and rouged and near to fainting with apprehension at what was soon to be done to him. The enslaved young royal had not even reached the well-guarded door to the king's guest quarters before the proud and always ready symbol of his manhood had shrivelled into a sorrowful version of itself as it sought to hide within the net-covered safety of his testes. Nevertheless, it would not have mattered even if it had risen up in all its glorious princely prominence, for this popular pillar of masculine flesh was not what the Spanish monarch desired.

It was not at all uncommon in the course of a single encounter for the king to deplete the entire contents of a bowl of fat before he had fully slaked his lust, not to mention fully slaked that of his weary young slave, who afterward became the subject of a good many chuckles when he had to pass before the Martinet's guests with the rouge-smeared mouth of his fundament gaping widely and wetly as a result of its kingly plundering. Even Prince Tristam's normally impassive peers in slavery could not resist indulging in a few silent snickers beneath their black masks as they observed their chagrined male counterpart returning from yet another turbulent session with the inadequately disguised king. For what possible disguise could have been adequate for a monarch of such distinctive girth?

Suzette, in particular, came to consider the prince's plight a source of considerable amusement. In her mind she had already relegated the young man to the category of the fair-fleshed Annabella, whose delicate aristocratic ways the marquis's former chambermaid had no tolerance for. Why should these highborn types not be used in the same manner as those lesser born? She was pleased by the lopsided gait Tristam had developed of late; a gait likewise shared by the similarly plundered Annabella, whose condition this tenured slave had been instrumental in creating. Suzette held her head up with pride. No one would ever catch *her* going about as if someone had stuck a fiery stake up her fundament.

By the close of the day the once amorous prince would endeavour to beg off from the remainder of his duties, his excuse being he did not believe himself capable of rising sufficiently to satisfy the passions of the Castle's female guests, many of whom had gone without a man's member for some months, if not years. This sudden disinterest in the needful passages of the fairer sex did not come about entirely as a result of mid-afternoon fatigue, however. Unable to hide the flagrant physical evidence of what had just transpired with the Spanish king, Tristam's humiliation might oftentimes prove so overwhelming the young royal could not bear to perform even the simplest act of fleshly commerce upon these elegant ladies of title, let alone be made the recipient of their bemused gazes and behind-the-hand snickers. Unfortunately, the slaves of tenure beneath whose supervision Tristam had been placed showed their aggrieved charge not a moment's sympathy or leniency, since no such luxuries had ever been afforded them. It was not his place to nurse his wounded pride, or indeed his wounded backside. Like his golden-ringed superiors in slavery, Tristam had been brought to the Castle to serve, and such service consisted of whatever the Martinet's guests desired at all times.

Despite his undesired position as the king of Spain's most favoured slave, the prince considered himself fortunate in one respect – that the king had not seen fit to require him to have the ring of iron removed from the prepuce of his manhood, a procedure that was customarily undertaken by one of the senior slaves at the request of a guest who yearned for the type of servicing only an unencumbered male member could provide. Although Tristam would have preferred to forgo this restrictive wearing of the ring altogether, its unauthorised extrication was strictly forbidden, and any attempts to embark upon such an enterprise were certain to be met with a punishment chosen and instituted by a slave of higher rank.

Such punishments went on at the Castle more often than might have been thought, with the Martinet turning a blind eye to this special form of privilege by those who served beneath his roof. The most favoured penalty would generally be that of the disobedient party's absolute and unquestioning sexual servitude to his or her enslaved superior for a period not to exceed seven consecutive nights. Thus far, the handsome young heir to the English throne had managed to elude these punishments, for he had heard that even the slightest effort to interfere with the iron ring's seemingly impervious clasp could have resulted in a week's worth of carnal homage to those who had been granted their prestigious rings of gold. Of course, there were some at the Castle who had already discovered the secret to freedom, only to learn that the use of this freedom brought either punishment, or allowed them to prey upon others in the same situation as themselves.

Tristam had the latter outcome in mind. Using the covert darkness of night to shield himself, he tinkered in silence with this diminutive tool of restraint, hoping the impressive shaft of his manhood might once again regain its liberty, even if only for a few precious moments. Unlike those at the Castle whose feminine charms had captured his fancy, the prince's motive for parting company with the intrusive iron ring had little to do with comfort and everything to do with desire. For he very much wished to sample the temptingly rouged fundaments belonging to some of the Martinet's female slaves, especially the fair-fleshed slave with the highbred ways whose pierced and protracted clitoral flesh gleamed with such succulent pinkness that it made its enslaved royal admirer salivate just to think of it. Perhaps he might taste these tender morsels with his tongue before tasting the other, more forbidden morsel with his member, since this would make his triumph over the girl all the sweeter. For there could be no more delicious victory than having her quaking in climax as he launched himself deep into her lovely bottom.

Prince Tristam often wondered if they might have made one another's acquaintance back home in his native land, for he felt certain the flaxen-haired female slave was as blue-blooded and English as he was. Had they perchance dined together at the duchess's stately home in the country? Or might it have been the residence of the nearly insolvent earl? Sadly, Tristam would neither be granted an opportunity to discover the slave girl's aristocratic identity nor the treasures of the brightly rouged mouth of her bottom, at least not until he could rid his member of its shameful shackle.

Like the other young men and women who had found themselves thusly encumbered, simple determination would not be enough for Tristam. The tiny ring of iron imprisoning the retractable lip of his hungering manhood had been constructed in so clever a fashion that it was virtually impossible for the wearer to remove it, which appeared to explain why none of the male slaves ever went about with their members happily unhampered, and why none of the female slaves could be spied without their more dainty equivalents stretched and splayed for all to see. Prince Tristam believed with masculine surety that it was a far less grievous matter for his enslaved female peers, whose intimate piercings could not have conceivably interfered with the normal functions of their daily lives or the libidinous encounters they were made to participate in. If anything, their be-ringed circumstances served to enhance the natural beauty of their feminine landscape, allowing a discerning gentleman like himself to fully appreciate the finer intricacies usually kept discreetly hidden within a young lady's densely haired nether lips. In this respect, young Tristam unknowingly shared a companionable kinship with his mysterious jailer, the Martinet.

Little did the enslaved heir to the throne suspect that this enforced wearing of the ring was likewise viewed as a most unwelcome and uncomfortable intrusion by the very same slave whose pierced female parts he greedily admired and desired, in fact, so great an intrusion that the afflicted wearer had once acted to temporarily free herself when away from the watchful eye of those whose responsibility it was to keep her bound. As a result, the seven nights of punishment Tristam had heretofore managed to avoid instead befell the fair-featured slave girl whose lusty fundament the prince one day planned to ravish.

In what had proved to be a futile effort to loosen the iron rings stretching and straining her delicate clitoral flesh, Annabella would be caught in the act by Suzette, who did not take kindly to her highborn charge's attempts at rebellion. Perhaps if the Martinet had made the discovery, a less grievous punishment than that which this stringent slave of tenure meted out might instead have resulted. Alas, such would not be the case.

Night after night, the beautiful young daughter of the English earl found herself being summoned to the Castle training chamber, where she was forced to pleasure the marquis's former chambermaid to the fore and aft with her tongue, and all of this after having already spent the day doing so with the insatiable mounds and backsides of the Martinet's male and female guests alike. Annabella's overworked tongue received its preliminary inspiration via a highly invigorating course of smacks upon her bottom by Suzette, whose palm demonstrated no mercy. By the time this slave of tenure had finished, the shapely hills of the girl's buttocks glowed bright red, the conflagration spreading to her upper thighs in variegated fiery streaks. It came as a mixed blessing that Annabella was so rarely required to be seated during her work at the Castle.

During that interminable week of punishment, Suzette showed herself to be a most demanding taskmaster as she ruthlessly fitted Annabella's overused fundament with the hated wooden training tool that put even the king of Spain's majestic manhood to shame. In order to make certain the device could not be dislodged, Suzette secured its base with an extra wide strap designed especially for this purpose, thereby keeping the girl permanently plugged. This was not done for the sole purpose of cruelty, however. In having been made the recipient of the flesh-and-blood variety during the course of the day, Annabella found the training member's unyielding and superfluous introduction to be so vexing that she was inspired to shimmy about during the performance of her oral duties upon the slave who enslaved *her*. This inadvertently provided the splayed contours of Suzette's womanly parts with additional stimulation, to say nothing of the rapturous benefits to be gained by a thorough investigation of her fundament. For it was the latter to which the chambermaid demanded the greatest devotion, knowing as she did that this would be the most shameful act to one of Annabella's class. Not even the despotic Madame Legros could have conceived of so circuitous an avenue to pleasure.

Suzette would scold the girl endlessly, realising full well she demanded the impossible, yet nevertheless wishing to challenge her young charge through fear and intimidation. 'Thy unworthy tongue must reach deeper,' she hissed, thrusting her own forcefully parted hind cheeks into Annabella's flushed face, feeling the velvety tongue inside her straining to accomplish the unnatural task set for it. 'Art thou deaf? I said deeper!'

And so it would be for each of the seven nights of Annabella's special punishment. After her black-masked and golden-ringed tormentor had finally been sated, Annabella was ordered to part her trembling thighs so the exacting Suzette could remove a single link from the pair of slender chains crisscrossing the barbered terrain of her patrician ward's pale mound. At the conclusion of her week of punishment, the wings of Annabella's clitoris were drawn as tightly as the strings upon her cherished lute, forcing into full and delicious exposure the tiny scarlet mouth of her sex, which had been pulled open to form a startled O; an O that many at the Castle longed to fill with nearly as much enthusiasm as its rouged neighbour to the rear... although the fulfilment of such a desire had been strongly discouraged by the Martinet, who did not wish to return the blue-blooded females placed in his care to their families with swollen bellies.

Like the master of the Castle, Prince Tristam had come to consider this enforced disclosure of the intimate parts of a female so appealing, especially the freshly exaggerated contours belonging to Annabella, that he planned to make the practice the law of the land when he became king.

If he became king.

In the meantime, the enslaved prince had other difficulties to concern him, and these difficulties did not merely involve the unwanted attentions of the Spanish king but also the unwanted attentions of a fellow slave. Possessing as he did the refined and fair features often characteristic of his countrymen, Tristam would unwittingly find himself being pursued by the ruffian horse thief, Frederico. According to slave gossip, the woman suspected to be the queen of Flanders had taken quite a fancy to the swarthy young Spaniard, a fancy he did not reciprocate but nevertheless acted upon, as was his function. Although the lady had always made certain to don a mask during her many visits to the Castle, and during her many trysts with Frederico, most everyone had guessed her regal identity, for no mask could have disguised the Flemish queen's buxom bulk. Just as no mask could have disguised the king of Spain once he had released his infamous member from his breeches to lay claim to his slave of preference. Unfortunately for Prince Tristam, it was *he* who had been made the king's slave of preference, and now it appeared he had become the slave of preference for still another.

In the close velvety darkness of the hot Spanish night, this common stable hand fitted himself firmly and with undaunted persistence against Tristam's back so he could perform the special act he so often performed upon the

Flemish queen. However, unlike in previous such encounters, Frederico derived a good deal more pleasure from the pert and muscular backside of the English prince than he had ever enjoyed at the floppy-cheeked and generously dimpled bottom of her majesty. As it happened, Frederico would not be required to travel very far to pursue his pleasures, since both he and Tristam shared a tiny bedchamber as well as a tiny bed.

The future king of England would be made to suffer these forbidden interludes in silence and resignation. Were it not for the fact that he was unable to call upon the authority of his position, Tristam would have ordered the other man's swarthy neck fitted with the hangman's noose. Instead he lay motionless as Frederico firmly grasped his royal victim's pale shoulders, only to insert his rigid member into the enslaved young prince's exhausted buttocks just as the king of Spain had done earlier in the day. Its highly intemperate usage on the part of the Spanish monarch made the act all the more painfully disgraceful, and Tristam soon found himself squealing softly and shamefully into the brown grassy-smelling palm that had closed over his mouth.

'You accept me most hungrily,' the Spaniard murmured with cruel sarcasm into Tristam's flinching ear. 'Did you not receive enough of a filling today?'

There appeared to be no escaping these unnatural overtures since all slaves, regardless of tenure, were required even while sleeping to wear the stiff girdle of hide at their waists. Thus the straps attaching to it remained fitted snugly in place along the smoothly barbered insides of Tristam's muscular bottom cheeks, keeping them widely parted, and leaving the well-exploited opening between them readily available for any ingress. Although this bridle would likely prove to be a major convenience for the time when he might finally steal an opportunity to force his attentions upon the similarly harnessed backside of the fair-fleshed slave whose rouged female parts haunted his dreams, never had the prince dreamed a similar ingress would be perpetrated upon himself by another slave, to say nothing of a slave of common blood.

Perhaps he should have tried harder to fight off his swarthy and sizably endowed aggressor, who had surely taken his lack of struggle as acquiescence. However, Tristam entertained no illusions when it came to matters of manly prowess, particularly when any attempts toward this prowess were doomed to be met with even further brutality by his attacker, who might be inclined to wield his thick weapon several times within a single night. Regrettably, the prince had never been blessed with a very brave nature... except, of course, when it came to exerting himself with the ladies, whose elegant skirts would always be raised easily and eagerly for him. When one was heir to the throne, there was always a host of others willing to do one's bidding and suffer one's wounds whenever there transpired an incident of insult or affront. Only now such persons were painfully absent, leaving the enslaved young royal at the mercy of king and horse thief alike. Perhaps Tristam was more like his weakling brother than he wished to think. Or perhaps it was simply a matter of silently submitting to his lowly persecutor so the other two enslaved males who shared their tiny quarters would not learn of what transpired in the adjacent bed, and thus could not speak of it to others.

For he could not bear to think that one of these others would surely have been the beautiful flaxen-haired slave girl, from whose pearly pink ears the prince wished more than any to hide the details of his recent indignities. Although he might not always have been used like one, he was still a man and therefore in possession of a man's pride. Hence, as Frederico continued to thrust and grunt his way in and out of Tristam's cringing backside, the quiescent recipient of these thrusts and grunts found himself pondering issues of more immediate importance, namely the question of how his unwanted paramour had managed a successful removal of the ring of iron that kept a slave's member out of service. Many a time had Tristam toiled furtively beneath the bed linens to free himself so he might do to the Castle's fair-fleshed female slave what was presently being done to him, but to no avail.

To keep from going out of his mind – for the future king feared he would soon be fit only for the madhouse if these criminal couplings by his swarthy bed-mate continued – Tristam turned his troubled ruminations toward more pleasant matters, such as the slave girl of his desire and the rouged mouth of her fundament, whose distinctive charms had been made clearly visible to the admiring eyes of nobleman and slave alike. How delightfully it always twinkled after receiving an enthusiastic visit from one of the Martinet's gentleman guests, or indeed from several gentleman guests. It did not even require any further enhancement of the rouge, for by evening this well-prized portal of pleasure had taken on all the brightly hued brilliance of a ruby. Unlike her royal admirer's almost exclusive appropriation by the Spanish king, the earl's daughter would be presumed upon by many, a fact that occasionally benefited the prince.

When his services were not required elsewhere, Tristam would be enlisted to accompany the popular Annabella during the performance of her duties, a demanding task but also a worthwhile one. The masked heir to the throne had come to be granted the extreme good fortune to be placed in the position of assistant as the fair-fleshed female slave serviced a gentleman guest in the favoured manner. Tristam's responsibilities generally consisted of seeing to it the gentleman was not distracted from his pleasure by having to pause and lather himself with handfuls of fat when the necessity for additional lubricant arose. For this function Tristam could be counted upon to stand discreetly by, where he waited with a pounding heart and a member as rigid as that of the guest whose activities he monitored, for this dorsal plunderer to signal with a telltale dip of the head that further lubrication be administered.

In his duties Prince Tristam had been taught well. Rather than touching the fleshly object in need of lubrication, he wisely acted to spare the gentleman from any additional discomfiture by applying the rich yellow fat directly onto and into the gaping mouth that had for the occasion already been freshly clystered and rouged. Although he would have preferred taking more time in his work so the divinely bottomed Annabella might experience the full benefit of her humiliation by having Tristam's knowing fingers probing her over-plumbed fundament, he had been given strict orders never to interfere with a guest's pursuit of pleasure. So he performed his task with a rapid expertise, all the while making certain this female slave knew precisely *whose* grease-slathered fingers her hind parts briefly entertained by offering her a purposeful wink from beneath his black mask.

As the future king lay passively upon his side, mentally savouring these deliciously stolen moments with the masked maiden who had been made into an object of carnal enjoyment for men much less worthy than himself, Tristam discovered his member was growing demandingly hard. He felt his face flush with humiliation, for this had transpired while the Spanish horse thief was in the midst of stealing forbidden pleasures from his captive backside. Tristam's manhood fought valiantly to escape from its confining ring of iron, the pierced purple flesh of the prepuce retracting so far down over the thickening shaft that its resilience brought to mind the artificially stretched clitoral flesh of the Castle's female slaves. This unbidden image of a pair of vibrant pink wings branching gracefully upward and outward, like the flaps of a seraglio tent being opened in welcome, was more than the enslaved royal could bear. To Tristam's supreme shame, his imprisoned manhood chose this inopportune moment to discharge its hot frothy desire into his palm, just as Frederico's own hot frothy desire was likewise discharged into his princely prey's smarting rear passage. On that night, both young men would be smothering their masculine groans of pleasure into their pillows, the feathers of which absorbed most, but not all, of the sound.

For at the Castle, not even the pillows could keep a confidence.

An Unwanted Discovery

After spending so many nights in the shameful clutches of the Spanish horse thief and seeing no conceivable end to them in sight, Tristam realised deep down to his degraded soul that these after hour pleasures taking place in the slaves' quarters were certain to remain a secret no longer. Word of Frederico's illicit bedchamber dalliances with the young prince quickly spread through the entire wing of the Castle housing the slaves. Although neither participant ever spoke of what transpired during these nightly events, the two slaves who shared their cramped quarters had undertaken no such vows of silence. On the contrary, these former domestic servants spoke openly and gleefully of the curious sounds coming from the wildly creaking bed of their enslaved male peers, adding provocative details where none were needed.

Alas, petty jealousies afflicted those of every station. Like Tristam's privileged female counterpart, the earl's daughter, nearly all who had been placed into sexual servitude by the Martinet eventually found themselves in some way resentful of the highly appealing exterior and refined manner of the English prince. For this manner made it painfully apparent to those of inferior blood that, despite the commonly held slave-issue accoutrements of his black mask and leather bonds and the rings of iron piercing his tender flesh, this fair-featured young man was unquestionably above them.

Therefore, it would not be very long before Tristam

noticed he had once again become the unwitting victim of sneers and snickers. But unlike the aristocratic titters that usually plagued him after an afternoon tryst with the randy Spanish king, these plebeian expressions of amusement came directly from his fellow slaves. Believing his personal honour to have been seriously compromised by his brutish bed-mate, Tristam decided upon an unprecedented stroke of bravery to get to the heart of the matter by confronting Frederico outright, even going so far as to challenge the horse thief to a duel, the proposal of which would be met by mocking laughter; no one had ever heard of the Martinet's slaves engaging in such chivalrous activities as duels. Nevertheless, it soon became apparent to the defamed prince by means of Frederico's natural disinclination toward chatter (for rarely had anyone heard him utter a syllable during the entire time he had been in servitude at the Castle) that the Spaniard had not spoken of their contemptible nocturnal nuptials, which could only have meant it had been through entirely different mouths that Tristam's disreputable secret had been set free. There were only two other residents in the Castle who could possibly have been privy to these nightly activities, and they occupied the next bed over.

Humiliated and angry and hungry for vengeance, Tristam considered securing a poison from the Martinet's cellars. He had heard that in addition to housing a whole variety of wine and spirits, certain deadly preparations were kept there for the control of household pests. And indeed, the prince could think of no greater household pests than the pair of slaves who shared his and his swarthy bed-mate's tiny quarters. Perhaps he might manage to place a few drops of the poison onto the womanish lips of these gossipy catamites while they lay asleep in their bed, or slip it into their food when their attention was directed elsewhere. So desperate was the disgraced young royal to silence these wicked scandalmongers that he even gave serious thought to enlisting the criminally proficient aid of Frederico, since it had been his unnatural actions that had created the situation in the first place.

Yet as Tristam mentally formulated his plan for revenge, he came to accept the complete futility of it. By now the damage had been done; no doubt the entire household, and in all likelihood even the Martinet himself, knew that the future crowned head of England had been made the slave of another slave.

Unbeknownst to Tristam, predatory situations amongst slaves were not altogether unheard of at the Castle, and such news might have cheered him considerably. What salacious delight he would have taken in the knowledge of Annabella's recent week of enslavement at the punitive hands of Suzette, the details of which would have brought him many moments of private rapture, not to mention further inspiration for the delicious moment when he and his temporarily liberated member finally caught her alone. However, since these acts of subjugation generally presented themselves in the form of a senior slave's personal procurement of a common slave – such fringe benefits coming exclusively to those of tenure and therefore transpiring in the customary domain of the training chamber – events of this nature tended not to be a topic of discussion among those of lesser status. Had it occurred to Tristam that he too could have compelled this divinely fleshed daughter of nobility to do his sexual bidding, he might have applied himself with a good deal more enthusiasm to his position of servitude and, like Suzette, found himself being rewarded with his own shiny rings of gold. Yet instead he was placed in the most humiliating position of all as the nightly plaything of a common horse thief.

Having been brought up to respect the proper workings of justice, Prince Tristam believed that had the Martinet been made aware of these criminal doings he would not have stood for such hubris on the part of a slave, especially a lowly slave like Frederico. The presumed upon young royal could not even imagine the terrible punishments that would have been meted out for one who dared to behave in the fashion of his societal betters, especially when those betters were aristocratic gentlemen who indulged themselves in the same method of pleasure as that which the cheeky Spaniard indulged himself in the dark of night and beneath the bed linens. It was an accepted fact that such pursuits were the prerogative of the upper classes, not the lowly born, which only made Tristam all the more astonished by Frederico's behaviour. Unfortunately there was nothing the future king could do when it came to informing on his tormentor, since it had been expressly forbidden for a slave to speak to the Martinet unless bidden to do so. And it appeared most unlikely that the aggrieved prince would ever be so bidden.

As for the pair of slaves whom Tristam strongly suspected had been the catalysts for so much laughter at his expense, they too had once served as the bedtime prey of the muscular Spaniard, although that did not make them any more sympathetic to this newcomer's plight. Prior to the imperially born Englishman's arrival at the Castle, the two young men who shared Frederico's quarters had themselves become the primary focus of the horse thief's sodomistic attentions, with them both oftentimes being used at the same time as the nimble

Spaniard switched from one to the other without even stopping to catch his breath. All this quickly changed after the fair-featured male slave with the better-than-thou mannerisms arrived to share their small bedchamber. It was not that the two particularly lamented the loss of Frederico's crude nightly probing; like their delicately fleshed brother in slavery, they had already received more than sufficient of such hind-ward activities during the day and well into the evening hours to accustom them to it. The fact that they could at last be allowed to sleep through the night unmolested would in the beginning prove a most agreeable situation for both. However, it was a situation that shortly turned into a growing resentment toward this newly arrived *parvenu*.

Human nature can be a very strange thing indeed, especially if one discovered him or herself living under the licentious punishment of the Martinet. Although Frederico's former victims had not exactly welcomed his attentions, his attentions had not gone entirely *unwelcome* either. Males of their particular cast derived considerable flattery from the amorous overtures of another of their sex, even more so when such overtures happened to be put forth by one of youthful vigour and pleasing exterior. Sadly, gentlemen callers to the Castle in possession of such qualities were great rarities. Hence with the arrival of Tristam, the two slaves saw themselves being rudely usurped by one who clearly considered himself their social better. Had they only known of this interloper's regal identity, they might have endeavoured to curry his favour, their return to their former posts being in some doubt. Of course, it was highly unlikely the sticky-fingered servants of a titled Norse family would have been familiar with the members of the English monarchy; the telltale pinkish-brown mark of the royals visible on Tristam's upper lip had about as much significance to them as a satisfied belch at the supper table.

Thanks to the pernicious gossip that had been set into unstoppable motion by his envious peers in enslavement, the appealing young prince discovered he had now been marked in yet another way, a way that had nothing to do with iron rings or bands of hide. Having been associated with the illicit nightly tampering of the coarsely handsome Frederico, Tristam began to gain an unwanted reputation at the Castle as being a lover of his own sex. Even the king of Spain had taken to smiling at him in a manner that implied they were cut from the same cloth.

Not surprisingly, it became increasingly difficult for Tristam to ignore the comments being whispered, not altogether discreetly, behind an aristocratic hand.

'Hark, there he goes...'

'Aye, the fair one... *there*...'

'Hast thou ever laid eyes upon such a gaping fundament?'

Were it not for the restrictive bands of his costuming, the young prince's ramrod-straight spine would have warped into a slouch as he slunk miserably past his aristocratic jeerers. If he could have gotten his hands on the Martinet's ivory-handled walking stick, he would have thrashed those who taunted him to within an inch of their privileged lives, then taken the stick to the muscular rear cheeks of the swarthy Spaniard until they burned with the same fire as that which now burned in Tristam's overused rear. Perhaps he might also apply it to the beguiling backside of the female slave whose own bottom so tormented his thoughts and fantasies, for he felt certain he had seen the eyes behind her black slave's mask brighten in amusement at the obviousness of his plight. How satisfying it would be to put forth a few punitive whacks of the stick upon that brightly rouged mouth before finally dipping into it!

With ever more frequency did the punished royal discover himself being assigned to the Martinet's older gentlemen callers, all of whom made no secret of the fact that they desired the pert-cheeked and readily available bottom of a handsome young man. Tristam's pleasant trysts with the fine ladies of title, whose charming daughters he had once engaged in improper associations back in his previous life, became less and less, until they ceased taking place altogether. How could it be that these aristocratic females should have suddenly lost all interest in their once-favoured slave's masculine prowess that they now considered it completely unnecessary to even request his company? For Tristam's courtly bows toward these perfumed and powdered personages came to be met by a not-so-subtle turning away of the head and a not-so-dainty wrinkling of the nose rather than the covetous grasping of the chain that attached to the iron ring piercing the retracting prepuce of his member, which had become renowned for lengthening itself impressively in the presence of females. Alas, the removal of the restrictive ring at the charming behest of a lady would now be undertaken at the brusque behest of a gentleman, since there were some who preferred the servicing of their own backsides to servicing the backsides of others. To the increasingly disparaged prince, this had been most unprecedented in his experience and therefore afforded a far greater affront upon his manly sensibilities, particularly when he was called upon to undertake such unnatural communions with the effete and flamboyantly masked

Sir Percival. For this gentleman guest's recently exercised fundament was extremely keen to graduate from Suzette's wooden training members to those of flesh-and-blood.

The noble Sir Percival showed himself to be as enthusiastically enamoured of Tristam's majestically curved manhood as the king of Spain was of Tristam's fundament, thereby officially designating the Castle's royal-blooded slave as an exclusive plaything of men. No longer would the prince hear himself being summoned into service for one of the Martinet's lusty female guests. For once a slave had been placed into this special category by way of his convenient duel usage – that being a gentleman guest's enjoyment of both a male slave's front and rear parts – he henceforward remained so until his sentence at the Castle had been served to completion. For Tristam, there could be no returning to the feminine pleasantries of earlier days. The strict rules set forth by the Martinet forbade crossing back to the other side once a male slave had demonstrated his propensity for servicing one of his own gender in every capacity. It would appear the raucous and public deflowering of the squealing Sir Percival – who had suddenly lost his fanatical desire for privacy by demanding the final act be carried out in the presence of his masked peers by none other than the enslaved prince himself – had gone and sealed Tristam's fate. One look at the fair-headed young slave's impressive member had been enough for Sir Percival to know that *this* was the fleshly specimen for him. The stern-mannered slave girl with the dark hair and the even darker temperament had not been practicing upon him with those divine wooden effigies in vain.

As he continued to endure the numerous indignities being foisted upon him by his own sex, Tristam would often catch himself envying the brutish Frederico for his frequent assignations with the well-fed personage of the Flemish queen, who seemed in no way cheated from her fleshly satisfactions despite the fact that her slave of choice was known to spend his nights pursuing the unwilling backsides of his fellow males in slavery. Strangely, this knowledge had no effect upon the Spanish horse thief's overwhelming popularity with the Castle's female guests. Nor did it relinquish him, as it had Tristam, to the exclusive sexual domain of men. Unfortunately, there was nothing the prince could do to win back his lost honour... unless, of course, he might somehow manage to get his hands on the beautiful Annabella, whose luxuriously rouged parts would surely grant him his desperately needed redemption. Perhaps he might finally receive his opportunity during festival week, since it was not unheard of for Castle slaves to revel in the same fashion as their masters. And Tristam had already waited far too long to indulge in revelry with the fair-fleshed daughter of the English earl.

Rousseaulet the Highwayman

Prince Tristam's hopes of redemption at the hands, and at the beguiling backside, of the finely fleshed Annabella appeared to be growing less and less likely with the passing of each day. As much as he wished to lay claim to the brightly rouged opening of her bottom, there were too many others at the Castle who felt similarly inclined, others the young royal in his present lowly status of slave could not possibly have contended against. No doubt if he had been allowed to assert his sovereign authority as the future king of England matters would have been very different. With his true identity finally revealed, Tristam felt certain the haughty young slave girl would have dropped into a servile crouch on the floor and begged him to take from her what he most desired, pleaded with him, in fact, until the tears streamed from her eyes so desperately did she long for him to fill her bottom.

By that time Tristam would have already done a fine job marking the pale cheeks being offered up to him with the Martinet's walking stick, perhaps even loosening the rouged harlot's nether orifice with the ivory handle so it would be all the more ready to absorb him. Regrettably, the risk of scandal to both himself and the English crown needed to take precedence over a silly competition between grown men to reap the physical pleasures of a woman. Prince Tristam was not so naïve as to think the man who controlled his destiny was incapable of causing damage, if thusly provoked. For it was becoming all too apparent to those who called the Castle home that none other than the Martinet himself had taken an interest in the beautiful daughter of the earl, an interest far exceeding that typically encountered in the custodial role of master to slave.

More and more could the Martinet be heard to have intervened in the assignment of Annabella to his titled guests. In fact, he would often go out of his way to pair her with those of more uncommon erotic tastes whose aberrant company even an experienced slave of tenure like Suzette preferred to avoid. Not surprisingly, some of the senior slaves began to suspect their mysterious master might be grooming the delicate looking girl for Castle tenure, if not grooming her for his own private use in future. Although the torch-lit rooms of the Castle were filled with secrets, they were not secrets easily kept. The Martinet's impassioned courtship of Lady Langtree had long been the stuff of gossip among slaves of tenure, many of whom had been present during the time of the affair. Why, not since the day of Her Ladyship's departure with her husband had the master of the Castle been known to have involved himself in similar engagements with a lady of quality, which meant that if the Martinet maintained a genuine personal interest in the flaxen-haired female slave whose identity only he was privy to, then her veins must have been in possession of some very patrician blood indeed.

The speculations indulged in by these increasingly resentful slaves were not without some basis in reality. It so happened the Martinet *did* have his expert eye trained on Annabella, whose remarkable progress beneath his roof filled him with pride. Although his successes with those he had enslaved were multitudinous, he often lamented with bittersweet melancholy over what might have been if some of the comely young ladies dispatched to his care had not fallen into less accomplished hands, never even reaching the Castle. As for those who had completed their sentences of servitude and been sent on their way, he could only wonder about their fates. For in the course of their journeys, any one of these females might have become the property of the notorious highwayman, Rousseaulet.

Over the years the Martinet had heard of several young women whose coaches had not returned them home at the designated time, if they had even been returned at all. Although he might not have been able to save every one of them, he believed that through his actions he might manage to prevent such an unlawful acquisition from happening to the beautiful Annabella. For how could she fall prey to Rousseaulet and his band of thieves if she never left the Castle?

It was a known fact that the dusty and desolate roads of the land offered great danger to a traveller, especially when that traveller was an unsuspecting young woman journeying on her own without a chaperone. The drivers of their coaches tended to offer very little in the way of resistance when confronted by a masked gang of knife-wielding robbers. Not being men of honour, they valued their own lives far more than the life of some stranger who rode in their coaches, even if that stranger was a woman. Considerably more road-wise than their inexperienced female fares, these coachmen maintained no doubt that the highwaymen who obstructed their way would not hesitate for an instant to slit their throats if they dared to protect a lady's valuables, to say nothing of her precious honour. Whether the passenger be lowly housemaid or highbred princess, the terror-stricken drivers of their coaches would swiftly step aside, if not go running off altogether, the musket and dagger and the angry masked faces of those brandishing them serving as an excellent deterrent for any foolhardy acts of heroism these fellows might once have undertaken in the more impetuous days of their youth.

In the unlawful world of highwaymen where a young woman could go missing without a single witness to the act, or at least a witness willing to step forward, Rousseaulet came to distinguish himself by his numerous conquests over those who innocently travelled along what he considered to be *his* roads. Needless to say, he acquired a good deal more than the mere bijou or ducat over his successful career. For with the continuing popularity of the Castle, and the increasing number of guests requiring the special kind of entertainment only the Martinet could provide, Rousseaulet the Highwayman would make a most interesting discovery – more and more young ladies were travelling the roads, young ladies of appealing face and figure who went about for the most part unescorted. Obviously, the cowardly drivers of their coaches, who when blinded by the deadly glitter of a blade would rather have relinquished their own mothers than forfeit a single drop of their precious blood, were no obstruction.

This was precisely what Rousseaulet the Highwayman would be counting on when he and his men moved in to surround a lone coach whose tottery rear wheels sent up a trail of choking dust like a beckoning banner in the barren Spanish landscape. His sharp cry of 'Everybody out!' would echo through the empty countryside, as would his guttural laugh at the haste with which the coach's terrified female occupant climbed out, nearly tripping on her long skirts. Although he had succeeded in amassing enough

160

treasures to give up on this looting of coaches altogether, Rousseaulet had in recent days happened upon treasures of an altogether different kind. And somehow these treasures all appeared to be linked to the very same series of roads, a series of tenuous threads of grey rubble crisscrossing the land from northwest to southeast, which he now made his personal business to keep watch over. For unlike the newly minted coins of gold or the strands of brightly polished gems that usually passed his way, the treasures Rousseaulet the Highwayman desired to procure became those of the fleshly female variety.

With his continued surveillance of the roads and those who travelled them, it was only a matter of time before it came to Rousseaulet's notice that the shapely passengers of the coaches heading south-eastward in the direction of Cordoba, and consequently in the direction of the Castle, tended to be of a timid and innocent sort. Hence they required a considerable amount of time and effort when working beneath their grudgingly lifted skirts, time and effort the busy highwayman did not possess. The important business of relieving unsuspecting travellers of their valuables needed to take precedence above all else, even a friendly, albeit brief transaction of the flesh.

Yet for every problem there was a remedy just waiting to be discovered, and for Rousseaulet, this remedy was to waylay coaches whose young ladies were journeying in a westerly direction and thus *away* from the Castle. For strangely enough, the solitary female passengers of these coaches seemed to be very much the opposite of their easterly moving peers. Not only did these comely travellers offer far less in the way of protest once it had been made apparent exactly what Rousseaulet and his randy gang of thieves desired from them, but also their capacity for the successful fulfilment of masculine desires would be most proficiently and deliciously demonstrated.

A fellow of scrupulous vigilance, it had not escaped Rousseaulet's sharp eye that this copious capacity to offer even the most rapacious of men seemingly unlimited pleasure bore a direct relationship to a specific physical feature these lone travellers all appeared to have in common. Although a feature charmingly unique to women in general, it was one that had for some mysterious reason become strikingly pronounced in the women Rousseaulet encountered journeying westward. A perplexing coincidence, indeed, and one that inspired much in the way of merriment from Rousseaulet and his band of highwaymen as they reaped the lusty benefits this feminine heraldry provided.

No sooner had a female passenger stepped down from her coach then Rousseaulet would brusquely order, 'Up with your skirts, my lady!' for he could hardly wait for the festivities to begin. Never in all his years of experience with women had the highwayman encountered such an astonishing pageantry of clitoral flesh beneath an upraised skirt. Normally the bashful little appendage preferred to keep itself modestly hidden from view within its attendant mass of silken curls, or at least hidden from view until the salaciously curious Rousseaulet had forced the tremulous pendant into friendly exposure by introducing his thumb against the plump female lips within whose pulpy pink walls it had long been afforded a peaceful and unremarkable domicile. However, it appeared that these ungallant unveilings of the past would no longer be required. Not only did the highwayman discover the anticipated mass of curls to be conveniently absent in these westerly moving female travellers, but he also discovered the properly pursed lips of their sex parted in glistening eagerness of his rude inspection.

And what an inspection it would be as this distinctive organ of female pleasure the highwayman sought to harass with his fingertip rose audaciously outward from its hairless confines much like the upstanding member of its molester, the retracting hood bifurcating into two quivering points of tawny flesh, which contrasted dramatically with the ripe pink sinews it had left without shelter. The mere sight of this impressive garnish of womanhood inspired a shiver to slink sinuously down the spine of its male admirer, setting the liquid of his lust to boiling in his testes. The formidable size of the object should surely have qualified it as a freak of nature were it not for the fact that Rousseaulet had, through his criminal cleverness, brought into exposure several specimens of similar girth along the very same roadway, each offering tremendous promise of the pleasures to be had courtesy of its pretty proprietor. For whenever a young lady showed herself to be thusly endowed, not a single ingress would be barred to those who impeded her journey.

As simple men of simple imagination, Rousseaulet and his accomplices always commenced with a traditional roadside plundering of their victim's womanhood, often while her fearfully trembling driver watched keenly from the comfort and safety of his seat, his hand working frantically within his grubby breeches as each of the highway bandits took their turn with his hapless passenger. Grasping their female quarry's dainty ankles, and drawing them widely outward to better penetrate the hot little slit they sought, the highwaymen took considerable amusement from the pendulous appendage located between the woman's thighs as it flickered and flushed in

163

reciprocation of each hungry thrust of their greedy members.

'Aye, what is it you have there for us?' the men would query, their voices gruff with excitement and the strain of holding back the fluids threatening to burst prematurely forth from them. For prior to joining up with Rousseaulet, many of these men had been required to offer payment in return for such services, which were usually hurried and unsatisfactory.

As for their darkly handsome leader, issues of fleshly commerce had never really presented themselves, since rarely were Rousseaulet's carnal demands ever met with dissent. Nor were they likely to be in these dusty roadside encounters with the lone female passenger of a commandeered coach, a passenger finally making her way happily homeward from what had proven to be a lengthy period of enslavement at the Castle. Still ripe and open from her sentence of servitude, this former slave discovered herself completely incapable of offering resistance when being dragged from the coach and stripped of her cumbersome garments. Indeed, by this time she had forgotten *how* to resist, just as she had forgotten what acts of the flesh had been deemed unnatural and unseemly and therefore prohibited by righteous members of society; she had been left forever altered by the days spent beneath the Martinet's rule.

What might have seemed like a grave misfortune of fate to those whose yielding young bodies had been placed in sexual bondage showed itself to be anything but for the adventure seeking highwayman and his eager companions in crime. For while in the midst of enjoying the moist sweet passage of his victim's provocatively shorn womanhood, Rousseaulet – upon urging his booty onto her belly so he could reintroduce his member from this particular direction – came to uncover still another offer of sweet sanctuary. It was a sanctuary the likes of which he had never had cause to frequent, let alone any inclination to frequent. Of course, all this immediately changed for the opportunistic Rousseaulet thanks to the fortuitous disclosure of his detained traveller's well-conditioned hind portions. Never had he imagined so simple a repositioning of a woman during the act of love could have given rise to such deviant and deliciously unwholesome desires as those that had suddenly overtaken him.

For the uniquely altered attributes located to the fore were available in a slightly different form to the aft as Rousseaulet found himself being met with a pair of generously parted nether cheeks and, perchance even more of a delight, the gaping red mouth between them. It showed itself to be as thoroughly divested of hair as the traditional female parts, which within moments would come to be mercilessly ground against the dusty brown earth of the road as the lustful highwayman commenced with his hind-ward activities.

Suddenly, the hurried fornications of the past were no longer quite so rushed. To witness the relaxed manner in which Rousseaulet now worked, one would never have suspected the law was so close upon his heels, a fact that occasionally prompted his concerned cohorts to hasten him on with a few lewd cheers. The head highwayman had adopted a more analytical eye, a savouring of the stolen bounties at his full disposal. He would observe, rather than just *take*, since there was so much more to be learned and therefore enjoyed when all the senses were brought into play. For unless the newly initiated

Rousseaulet was seriously mistaken, the crinkled lip of overstretched flesh that provided access to this rear chasm of mystery had been adorned with what looked to be cosmetic rouge, a most inexplicable phenomenon, but one that encouraged its marauding admirer not to be in any way remiss in what he had come to consider his social obligations. No matter that these obligations had to be employed along the side of a road. As the unclaimed bastard son of a titled French aristocrat, it would have been terribly rude of the partially blue-blooded Rousseaulet to ignore the flirtatious come hither winks being directed his way with such bawdy and unladylike enthusiasm.

Not the sort to complain when confronted with the incredible good fortune that now presented itself to him, Rousseaulet the Highwayman happily withdrew the slick shaft of his manhood from the conventional female treasure-trove he had been in the midst of plundering, only to undertake an even more aggressive assault upon what would demonstrate itself to be an already well plundered treasure-trove... although its apparently intemperate usage by so many in no way lessened this recent inductee's pleasure. On the contrary, had it been possible for him to do so, the highwayman would have thanked these discerning gentlemen for their patronage. Unfortunately, a man in Rousseaulet's position did not always have sufficient time to undertake a leisurely deflowering of his female victim's untried fundament. Because of his continuous efforts to remain one step ahead of the law, the swiftly moving highwayman might all too often be required to leave the job only partially completed, a most unsatisfactory outcome for both parties.

Having been unfairly denied his proper birthright, Rousseaulet had become an ardent observer of those who believed themselves to be for the most part unobserved. Therefore, he considered himself a keen judge of character, especially when it came to the privileged individuals society had seen fit to place above him. It was no different whether his observations were made from the wrong side of a château window or while ripping the skirts from a female traveller's shimmying hips. For during the many roadside acquisitions undertaken by Rousseaulet and his trusted team of highwaymen, he could immediately distinguish a woman of common birth from a lady of pedigree by her manner and the quality of her possessions. As a general rule, he exercised somewhat more lenience with the former who, in his opinion, had already been punished enough by the lowliness of her birthright. As for the latter, he preferred to act in a far more cavalier fashion, since those of their ilk had too often shunned his company.

As the illegitimate son of a common French housemaid and the married gentleman of title who employed her and then subsequently dismissed her when learning of her ripe condition, Rousseaulet knew all about the injustices of birth. Although aristocratic blood coursed through his thieving veins, it had afforded him no special privileges in life, a fact that undoubtedly accounted for his choice of career and his lack of empathy toward those whom society deemed worthy of showering its favours upon. Therefore, in his ongoing quest for personal justice, it would be the female travellers of distinctly noble origins the hybrid-blooded highwayman shared with his pillaging peers at the edge of the road or in an adjacent field. Of course, if she demonstrated an aptitude particularly disposed toward matters of the flesh, like the lustily endowed women Rousseaulet had recently come upon, he might instead choose to spirit her away on his horse to enjoy at his leisure, or at least to enjoy until her charms had grown too familiar to hold any novelty, whereupon he and his men turned her loose. This granting of freedom was not done out of simple generosity, however, for recent experience had taught the men that there were many more of such uniquely featured females destined to pass their way, so there was no need to hold on to the ones they had already used to their satisfaction.

As a result, it was through Rousseaulet's acquisition and subsequent release that many a titled young lady suddenly, and with unexplained tardiness, reappeared within the once-chastising bosom of her family after a prolonged and mysterious absence, her newly unmasked eyes harbouring a strange and knowing glow, the cause of which concerned parents dared not enquire into. Just as they dared not enquire into the method of punishment meted out by the blue-masked man into whose hands she had been blindly placed.

It would be young women like these whose acquisition the highwayman desired most. Although Rousseaulet might not have known the nature of a lady's business for travelling unescorted along the lonely Spanish roads he kept watch over, he had learned prosperity did not always come in the form of jewels or gold. When the business of highway piracy was good, Rousseaulet could easily manage to procure for his own usage several of these highbred young ladies in a short span of time. Not surprisingly, he found himself growing extremely possessive of his female acquisitions and consequently less and less inclined to share them with his fellow highwaymen, whose peasant blood would surely have prevented them from fully appreciating the distinctive physical qualities that set these women apart from all the rest. Therefore, in an effort to rid himself of their unwanted masculine company so he could have such curious female charms all to himself, Rousseaulet began to concoct a series of superfluous tasks designed to take his men to more distant roads and, in the process, take them far away from his private harem in the deserted Spanish countryside.

How crowded the little cave of jagged rocks out of which he had made a convenient bedchamber would become when Rousseaulet detained his delightful female booty. Rather than granting them the freedom to continue on their way, he allowed avarice to get the better of him by keeping captive these westward moving travellers, since it would be they who had been thoroughly trained into performing every known act of the flesh, and even those sensual acts that were not known except perhaps in the most select of social circles. The Martinet had been most meticulous when it came to those who served under his domain, although it would have pained him greatly to realise the results of his hard work had ended their sentences by being pawed over by a common criminal in the Spanish dirt.

Be that as it may, the blue-masked personage of the Martinet meant nothing to Rousseaulet the Highwayman, who assumed quite naïvely that his roadside luck would continue indefinitely.

It might be imagined that the bug of curiosity would finally have bitten this lustful predator and plunderer, thereby compelling him to query his victims as to the exact circumstances that had brought about the uncommon physical characteristics it had been his pleasure to discover. For surely these ladies could not all be sisters sharing a peculiar family anomaly. If such a family of sisters did in fact exist, Rousseaulet would have happily relinquished his much coveted bachelorhood to marry into it. Yet instead he remained in blissful ignorance, passing his days by gazing upon the undulating wings of flesh left lewdly exposed by a pair of salacious lips prized immodestly open by some unseen force, relishing the sight of the thirsting muscle of his manhood as it sluiced into the ripe pink cleft below. If it happened the tireless highwayman had more than one such remarkably endowed female at his disposal, he would deliver his glistening member from backside to backside so it could know the forbidden taste of these chasms as well. Experience had already taught him to take his belt to the yawning mouth awaiting its turn in order to better heat it for the arrival of his erection, which meant he could be in the midst of plugging one young woman while simultaneously whipping another. He had yet to see one of these miraculously endowed girls flinch from the sharp snap of the weather-beaten hide, leaving him to conclude that their rouged openings had enjoyed such punishments long before he ever conceived of them.

It appeared that Rousseaulet the Highwayman had created for himself a paradise amidst the craggy rocks of the arid Spanish countryside, a paradise he did not wish to share; and such selfishness would eventually prove to be his downfall.

Just as Rousseaulet allowed himself to believe that his newfound felicity would last forever, so too did he cling to the vain belief that he would never be caught by the law. Yet as it has often been said, all good things must come to an end. By having successfully excluded his fellow highwaymen from partaking of the fleshly female pleasures procured by him, and kept exclusively to himself afterwards, Rousseaulet orchestrated his own undoing.

Feeling cheated and deprived by their leader, his partners in brigandage would thus be driven to seek a satisfying revenge. This vengeance took the form of their leader's unexpected apprehension along a dusty Spanish road as the coach whose progress he had chosen to interfere with proved to contain not one of his gloriously endowed and eager-bottomed young ladies, but a portly and moustachioed officer of the law.

With Rousseaulet the Highwayman now tucked safely away inside a Cordoba prison cell awaiting his appointment with the hangman's noose, his former associates in crime strove to continue his good work, albeit with far less success. For they had neglected to consider the obvious – that the handsomeness of the transgressor cannot so easily be dismissed when embarking upon lusty enterprises of the flesh.

Like Rousseaulet, much of the Martinet's success with the females placed in his care bore a direct relationship to his physical appeal. Regardless of a slave's distaste for a particular act, she had only to experience the fiery blue heat of the eyes behind his azure mask before she relinquished herself to the libidinous desires of a stranger. As this held true for the beautiful Annabella, so too did it hold true for those whose travel plans had been abruptly thwarted by Rousseaulet the Highwayman. Indeed, had the Martinet known that his once beloved Lady Langtree had undergone a similar such transformation of the spirit when finding her mode of transport being rudely intercepted by the intriguingly handsome Rousseaulet, he might not have pined so greatly and for so long over the loss of her companionship.

Lady Langtree had been in the process of journeying homeward from the Castle with her husband when it happened. The driver of their elegantly appointed coach had not even begun the precarious crossing of the Guadalquivir River before her ladyship became the temporary property of the ruthless and infamous highwayman. Not the sort of man to let his good efforts go to waste, Rousseaulet collected everything of value the terrified couple had in their possession, after which he boldly took it upon himself to use Lady Langtree in the very same fashion as that which she had previously begged the Martinet to use her, and all before the incredulous eyes of her husband.

Rousseaulet availed himself greedily of the lady's recently exercised fundament, throwing up her skirts and draping her languid form over the couple's travel trunk so he would not be required to grind the knees of his breeches into the dust as he worked. Although not rouged like so many of the others Rousseaulet had encountered along the same road, this particular female passenger's hind opening nevertheless possessed the same eager acceptance of his member. Even the gracefully sloping hillocks that rose upward to greet him with each vicious stab of his manhood into the dark valley between them seemed to invite some form of trespass, and the highwayman found himself unable to resist providing this pale landscape with a few slaps of the palm until there blazed a raging fire therein. He shocked even himself with the ferocity of his attack, the twin mounds provoking him until the flesh of his palm stung as if savaged by a swarm of angry bees. Rousseaulet could not help but be amused by the sputtering old fool he assumed was the woman's husband, although he noted with some disdain that the fellow made no attempt to portray the hero by intervening in this despoliation of his wife who, unless the experienced highwayman was sorely mistaken, appeared to be a willing enough participant. For one had only to listen to her satisfied grunts and groans to gauge the level of her pleasure.

Perhaps his lordship's astonished and affronted disbelief at the unseemly events transpiring along the roadside stemmed more from his mild-mannered wife's easy acceptance of this irregular encroachment upon her hind portions than from the actual banditry itself that was being perpetrated upon their small travelling party. Had Lord Langtree not known better, the Langtrees having been married for more years than he wished to count, he might have assumed his phlegmatic spouse had indulged herself in this manner many times before, for the frantic shimmying of her hips did not, at least in his eyes, imply a struggle. But surely such a crass supposition was sheer and utter foolishness on his part…

Long after the aristocratic Lady Langtree relived her earlier moments of ecstasy with the Martinet courtesy of the ruthless Rousseaulet the Highwayman, the master of the castle tossed restlessly in his bed at night fearing that what had befallen her ladyship might one day befall Annabella. With episodes of this nature taking place only miles from the fortified sanctity of the Castle, the Martinet vowed to do his utmost to keep his favoured slave under his erotic aegis for as long as possible, if not forever. For news of the felonious misfortunes that had assailed the lovely Lady Langtree, and so many others, eventually reached his ear and he could not bear to imagine the fair-fleshed daughter of the earl one day falling into coarse hands.

Yet even a man as powerful as the Martinet could not keep Annabella safe when such hands belonged to those at the Castle.

The Arrival and Departure of the Countess

Despite excited rumours of Rousseaulet the Highwayman's hanging, and the ongoing commandeering of coaches along the roads being conducted in far less successful fashion by his men, the routine at the Castle remained the same. The daily affairs of guest and slave had to be allowed to continue without interruption, especially since a further number of visitors would soon be risking the roads as they made their eager way to this rugged landscape once ruled by the Moors. For the preparations were already underway for the Festival of Saturnalia.

This festival was the event of the year, and one that had to take precedence over anything else that might have been consuming the Martinet's mind and his valuable time. Therefore, the safety of Annabella would become an issue he was forced to temporarily set aside. He had no reason to suspect someone with intentions even more criminal than those of the lawless highwaymen he so desired to protect her against dwelled beneath his roof in the guise of a common slave – a slave who had been made into a favoured plaything for his own gender. Had the Martinet not been so distracted with administrative matters, he might have sensed that life at the Castle had begun to change, including even his own.

Nearly everyone who mattered in European society journeyed to the Castle for this very special occasion. In order to accommodate as many of his esteemed guests as possible, the Martinet required a full year's notice of someone's intention to attend, with the sole exception of the king of Spain, whom he would not have dared to insult with the necessity of an advance booking.

Yet even if the Martinet had owned a whole slew of castles all throughout the Spanish countryside, they would not have been sufficient to accommodate the ever increasing demand he was met with each year. Hence, with as much diplomacy as possible, the Martinet did the best he could by making certain a guest would not be excluded from attending two years in a row. Of course, there were always the occasional gatecrashers who refused to accept his politely written apologies that the guest list was full, and who simply presented themselves at the Castle gates alongside the official invitees, secure in the aristocratic knowledge that *they* would not be turned away. Perhaps such a resoluteness to attend should not have been surprising, since even the Martinet himself looked forward with excitement to these seven extraordinary days of uninhibited feasting and revelry. For unlike in bygone years, this year the festival's typically aloof host had a bit of feasting and revelry he planned to indulge in as well.

Within weeks of the big event, trunks filled to overflowing with elaborate costumes began to be delivered to the Castle. Some of these trunks belonged to the soon-to-be-arriving celebrants, while others had come from the very best *costumier* in Paris, the contents having been ordered personally by the Martinet, who was known never to don the same costume twice. On any given day during festival time one might happen upon garments that were spangled, feathered, beaded and bowed, each more lavish and extreme than the next. Not so, however, for the Martinet, who preferred to rely more upon elegance than outrageousness. Unlike many of the gentlemen revellers who would be in attendance at the festival, he chose not to participate in the popular custom of attiring oneself in the garb of females. Although he never discouraged the practice in his aristocratic peers – for by doing so they not only desired to look like women, but to be *used* like women – the Martinet would permit no such epicene license when it pertained to himself. Any transgression of the norm, should he so desire to transgress it, needed to be conducted entirely in private, and with those who could be counted upon to remain discreet.

The Martinet's desire not to be made the subject of gossip or idle speculation would in particular extend to his dealings with the Castle's female guests, who were frequently known to make inappropriate overtures to their enigmatic host. Over the years, many a titled lady had endeavoured to get beneath the Martinet's elegant blue mask, not to mention inside his breeches, with some, such as the aforementioned Lady Langtree, having considerably more success than others. Therefore, it appeared likely that during the festival many more would attempt to do so in the atmosphere of total sexual abandon occasioned by the saturnalia. As a consequence, the Martinet, already anticipating one such female source of difficulty, was now more than ever obliged to place himself on his guard.

For this year it would not be her ladyship, whose despairing declarations of love had nearly unhinged the gentleman to whom they were intended, that would be attending the festival, but another of infinitely more persistent and exasperating character. Included among the many pedigreed visitors due to arrive for the festivities was the hedonistically favoured and smoothly sexed Prussian countess, the very same Prussian countess who had once flung herself without inhibition upon her host's bed, only to offer up an elaborate show of pleasuring herself to a noisy climax before the startled blue of her observer's eyes. Obviously, the Martinet preferred to avoid a repeat of such an embarrassing and compromising confrontation, however he could not very well dispatch a message to the countess informing her that she would not be allowed to attend festival week when nearly everyone in her social circle planned to be in attendance. Yet with the recent and unexpected death of her husband, the count, there were no longer any obstacles to get in the way of the countess's campaign to bed, and perchance even to wed, the Martinet.

It was no secret the Castle coffers were kept well filled with the generous and discreet bestowals of those members of the aristocracy who had been responsible for the life's blood of the Castle, namely the sponsorship of slaves. This ongoing revenue, coupled with his own family fortune, had made the Martinet even more eligible in the increasingly desperate eyes of the Prussian countess, whose own fortune from her uneventful marriage had dwindled to a sum scarcely sufficient to keep her in beauty patches. Unfortunately her late husband, who had been in the process of returning home on a ship he had filled with silk and spices from the Orient, had met a fatal end upon a jagged reef in unfamiliar foreign seas. Within seconds the ship had vanished beneath the emerald-green surface of the water, along with most of the couple's fortune. Thus the countess was left alone to count what little remained of a once vast cache of gold while simultaneously plotting how best to seduce her one hope of salvation, the fabulously wealthy Martinet.

It had become abundantly clear to the not altogether

bereaved countess that the master of the Castle required a woman of substance at his side, a fact she had frequently remarked upon whenever granted his cultured ear at supper. 'Sir, we are of remarkably similar tastes,' she would coo with breathless excitement, leading the Martinet's reluctant hand toward her powdered and heaving bosom as the two of them observed a tableside performance of buggery between a gentleman guest and one of the Castle's more comely female slaves. Perhaps now that Fate had finally seen fit to set her free from the bonds of matrimony, she and the enigmatic Martinet could rule over the Castle together...

A prepossessing woman in her own right, the countess did not pass her days without her share of lovers. The thought of having the widowed countess in one's bed should not have given rise to complaint by any man. She still retained much of the sweet blush of youth thanks to a life of pampering and ease, a life which by its very nature leant itself to an abundance of time to be directed toward one's appearance. Her beauty notwithstanding, the Martinet, having once complicated his life with the very lovely and very married Lady Langtree, did not desire to do so again, and the Prussian countess's new and disturbingly comfortable status of widowhood did nothing to convince him otherwise.

Upon being informed by the widow of the recent loss of her adventure loving husband, a loss that had undoubtedly left her severely wanting financially, his first, and indeed his very *accurate* inclination, would be to distance himself from the countess's society. The Martinet was nobody's fool; he knew the good lady was interested in a good deal more than the blue fire smouldering in his eyes.

Such self-preserving intentions do not always work according to plan, however, especially when underestimating the determination of a desperate woman. As one might have anticipated, the Martinet politely absented himself as much as possible from the countess's overly eager presence during the early days of the festival, hoping she would not take it upon herself to once again pay an uninvited and embarrassing call to his private quarters. In fact, he actually considered posting one of the more muscular male slaves at the door to his bedchamber, except none could be spared for such sentinel duty, the demands of the guests during festival week taking precedence over even the Martinet's personal requirements. As it happened, he need not have concerned himself about issues of security, for this time the clever countess had altered her tactics, as well as her place of seduction...

Having enlisted the expert aid of Suzette, who proved more than happy to relieve this privileged female of her proffered coins of gold, the Prussian countess would be gotten to endure the brief and not altogether painless process of piercing, only to be left shivering with forbidden delight upon seeing the two tiny rings of iron that had been driven into the virgin hood of her clitoris. The tawny tips flushed with heat at this unprecedented introduction, a heat that grew ever more fierce when the former chambermaid attached to the rings their accompanying chains, drawing them sharply upward so they could then be attached to the cinching girdle of hide now encircling the countess's naturally slender waist.

Suzette had not even completed her task before the widow was gasping excitedly for the removal of several links, for she suspected the Martinet would find her particularly appealing with her delicate clitoral flesh in the same severely elongated state as that of the Castle's female slaves. The countess even prevailed upon this senior slave to fit the shapely cheeks of her bottom with the supple bands of hide each slave was required to wear, demanding for them to be drawn so tightly within the inner crease of her buttocks that the heretofore unplumbed depths between them distended out like a mouth pursing daintily for a kiss. Although the countess wisely preferred to forgo what she considered an unnecessary and egregiously cruel piercing of the nipples, considering her own sharply pointed specimens sufficiently decorous in themselves, she was not above adorning herself with what so many at the Castle had come to consider perhaps the most severe indignity of all.

As a crowning touch, the Prussian countess procured a small pot of rouge so that when she returned to the privacy of her guest quarters she could embark upon a generous application of the substance to the exposed lip of virgin flesh designating the entrance to her fundament. The sensation of her own finger working in this unconquered territory excited the countess greatly, and she shuddered with delight at the thought of what would next be toiling in this region. The cosmetic was likewise extended to the luscious lips of her sex, the hair of which the widow had meticulously attended to only that morning with the blade, as per her usual custom. For good measure, she deployed the bright red ointment to the distorted and already reddened contours of flesh held provocatively asunder by their iron rings, thereby further complementing their newfound floridity. When she had finally completed the task she had set for herself, she went to stand before the looking glass, turning every which way to better examine her reflection. It was her vain opinion that the Martinet would be powerless to resist her now.

With the relinquishment of a few coins into the upturned palm of a male slave who informed her of his master's whereabouts, the Prussian countess found the Martinet in the sunny courtyard. He had been sitting in solitary concentration alongside the tinkling fountain perusing the Castle's recent financial figures, which had shown themselves to be most favourable. He hummed to himself with an uncharacteristic lightness of spirit, the tune faintly reminiscent of one that had been hummed to him in his boyhood years by a much-adored domestic. He enjoyed these quiet moments alone when he could concentrate upon the important business of running the Castle. Rarely did anyone visit the courtyard during the afternoons. The bright light of the Spanish day proved far too harsh for even the most debauched of Castle guests who, many having left behind their youthful physical primes, would have had a good deal more illuminated by the candid rays of the sun than he or she might have wished to have illuminated. Yet thanks to the determined widow of the count, the Martinet's highly coveted solitude would not last long.

All at once, the countess materialised before him in all her pierced and rouged finery. Her freshly powdered and perfumed bosom rose and fell with all the excitement of a young bride on her wedding night, and indeed, perhaps this was exactly how she viewed herself, the memory of her late husband's artless bedchamber grunts and ungainly heaving having by this time faded into the distant past. The top halves of her generously sized nipples, which the countess had carefully rouged and then pinched into spiky points to draw attention to them, peeked flirtatiously out from the snug satin bodice of her festival costume, the corset beneath having been laced extra tight to further flatter a waist not left thickened by childbirth. So constricting had this buttressing undergarment been made that the countess's greeting to the Martinet came to be expelled in a single gasp.

''Tis a very fine afternoon, sire,' she stated with the Castle's traditional slave-like deference, whereupon she gripped, without any sign of deference now, the grosgrain-trimmed hems of her skirts and raised them up well past the shapely convexity of her bottom.

By having conveniently forgone the wearing of the customary pannier, the exposure of her parts was all the more easily accomplished, which had, of course, been the lady's intention. So that the Martinet would not be mistaken as to her identity, for she had not been bold enough to go without her mask lest another guest of title encounter her, the Prussian countess had made certain before leaving her guest quarters that her trademark aigrette was fitted securely in place above her right ear. Its spray of diamonds glittered provocatively in the afternoon sunlight, leaving no doubt in the mind of the Martinet as to the identity of its intrepid owner.

The Martinet shot up from the stone bench encircling the fountain, astonished by this unprecedented interruption, for no slave beneath his roof would ever have presumed to embark upon such a rude trespass. Yet as he would quickly discover, this trespasser to his solitude was no Castle slave. As had been anticipated, he immediately ascertained the identity of his female intruder. Indeed, how could he possibly forget the fuss that had been made during the Prussian countess's previous visit regarding the supposed loss and miraculous recovery of her precious diamond aigrette?

Although his initial impulse was to lash out with stern words of reproof, the master of the Castle was first and foremost a gentleman, and therefore incapable of raising his voice to a woman. Not that he would have had a voice to raise in protest even if he had wished to. For the eyes behind the wax-stiffened silk of his mask brightened to the same distinctive shade of blue that framed them as they alighted upon the freshly pierced and dramatically splayed tableau of clitoral flesh the calculating widow now presented for his inspection. Her sensual button looked unusually flushed, even in the bright afternoon sunlight. Apparently, the rouge from the surrounding labial lips had been extended with copious generosity to this malleable feature as well, leaving the bifurcated appendage as radiantly red as a burning flame and undoubtedly as hot, if the Martinet knew the countess.

He discovered his tongue completely incapable of speech as the widow turned to face in the opposite direction, so her observer's blue gaze could now feast upon the immodestly distended mouth of her bottom, which glowed with the same brilliance as the ruby upon the little finger of his right hand.

To make absolutely certain the Martinet did not misunderstand her aspirations, the countess called with all her might upon this rouged ring of muscle to force itself outward and thus toward her handsome host, thereby deceptively broadening the maiden opening. She had practiced this exercise several times before her looking glass at home until she was able to make her virgin orifice look as open and ready as some of the fundaments belonging to the Castle's female slaves. She would have been extremely embarrassed if the Martinet had guessed

184

she had never before entertained a gentleman caller in this area.

If it had been the Prussian countess's intention to capture the Martinet's attention, she had most definitely succeeded. For never in all his years in running the Castle had he come upon a female guest who desired to have herself outfitted with the shameful accoutrements of a common slave. Aye, human nature would continue to be a source of amazement to him, as it would likewise be the guiding force that prevented him from bolting the Castle doors against those whose unique physical needs had driven them to seek out such a place in their quest for fleshly fulfilment. How tragic to think that the late count should have spent so much of his time dispatching the tool of his manhood from slave to slave, and seeming to single out those with the most common blood, when he'd had such luxurious bounties right in his own home in a woman of noble blood.

'Dost thou not wish to bestow a kiss upon this humble slave's unworthy fundament?' queried the countess in a markedly un-slave-like tone, her voice careening to a high and eager pitch on the last word. She could already feel the beginning stages of a climax building up just from the mere suggestion that the mysterious proprietor of the Castle might actually deign to place his lips upon her carefully rouged hind mouth. And perhaps she might do likewise to him, if he granted her the privilege. That should surely bind her to him, since how many men could claim to have been thusly worshipped by the likes of a beautiful countess? If anything, the lady knew that at this moment she was more beautiful than she had ever been in her entire life.

If the Martinet had only seconds ago been struck dumb

by the brazen and unexpected exhibition of the Prussian noblewoman's outspread bottom cheeks, he would discover by virtue of her salacious suggestion that he had misplaced his tongue completely, especially when the widow bent fully forward from her leather-girdled waist so he could observe her elegant fingers working frantically between her thighs, manipulating what they could manage to of the newly imprisoned flesh of her clitoris. She whimpered fitfully, gyrating her shapely hips in time with the hypnotic movements of her fingers, the wetness dewing the hungrily pouting sliver of her womanhood gleaming like a pearl in the sunlight. Had the countess known the Martinet's true Christian name, she would have shouted it with rapture to the blue Spanish sky above as she came.

Such a public act of self-stimulation did not result out of simple passion, however. It was all part of the countess's carefully crafted plan to offer the Martinet the most striking rear vista possible. In fact, ever since the death of her husband, she had spent many long hours posing before the looking glass so she could determine which would be the very best view – the view destined to ensure a successful seduction of the handsome and wealthy master of the Castle. The countess was not entirely indisposed toward a little hard work, particularly when the reward was so great.

Yet let it not be said that the Martinet was so terribly cold in his demeanour as to be minus at least *some* restless stirrings inside his well-tailored breeches. The cunning widow of the count made a most alluring composition with the brightly rouged mouth of her backside flickering with pent-up desire for her gentleman host as she rubbed herself to a resounding climax, the naturally rose-lipped pussy conveniently adjacent to her anus raining its lustrous pearls of ecstasy onto the insides of her trembling thighs. The fiery blue heat of the Martinet's eyes upon her in this highly unladylike pose proved more than a woman like the countess could endure, hence any efforts to regain her feminine dignity would be irretrievably lost.

'Oh, sire, fill me with thy manly member!' begged the aggrieved widow, only to further astound her audience of one by forcing several of her quim-moistened fingers into the rouged and quivering mouth of her bottom.

Faced with the very real possibility of having still more of his valuable time taken up with the gracious fending off of this overly persistent female guest during the busy days of festival week, the Martinet found himself compelled to make a swift decision. It was either acquiescence, which would allow him in due course to return his attention to the figures in his financial ledger, or outright refusal, which would inevitably bring on a dramatic display of dejected tears, not to mention the continued dramatic display of flesh that now presented itself to him. It appeared the choice was, in essence, no choice at all.

With a sigh of indifference even the countess could not have mistaken for desire, the Martinet slowly unlaced the straining front of his breeches. The task proved somewhat more difficult than he had anticipated thanks to the unruly condition of his member, which had not indulged itself in such lusty activities in quite some time. It must also be remembered the widow was a woman of great appeal, an appeal made all the more eloquent by a particular rouged charm even a gentleman as jaded as the Martinet could not have ignored. Perhaps if he provided the brazen-bottomed countess with a most thorough and rigorous plugging, she might in future let him be. For it was his expert opinion, if the lack of accommodation afforded the countess's intrusive fingers was any indication, that despite this wanton display to the contrary, her fundament had never courted a gentleman in the manner in which he now found himself being wooed. Perhaps he would give the opportunistic widow a *real* reason for bereavement.

And there in the sun-drenched courtyard of the Castle, alongside the gaily tinkling fountain, the Martinet made good upon his plan. With the generous girth of his manhood thrusting hungrily out from the front of his breeches, he reached for his ivory-handled walking stick, which had up until now been resting at his side. However, it would be resting no more. Taking expert aim he brought it down upon the outthrust buttocks presented to him, eliciting from their unsuspecting owner an astonished cry and the beginnings of a protest.

'Sire, I had not intended for—'

'Slave, thou shall not speak to thy master,' admonished the Martinet, all at once genuinely angry at this unprecedented interruption to his schedule. If a guest desired to be used like a slave, who was he to deny her? Ergo, he wielded the stick with increasing impunity, alternating from left to right so each of the countess's shapely bottom cheeks would get its due. When they had at last attained a shade evocative of spilled blood, he took to punishing the greedy opening between them, cracking the stick at the wantonly rouged mouth until it actually appeared to plead with him to stop so frenziedly did it twitch and convulse.

Only then did the Martinet finally launch himself with one ferocious stroke into its virgin depths, not bothering to avail himself of the carafe of rich oil that had been replenished by a servant only that morning and now sat unused within a finger's reach. Indeed, so furious were the Martinet's movements that his shoes nearly slipped in the clear droplets of moisture that had rained onto the tiles from the mouth of his own impatiently waiting member.

Later that evening, when the Prussian countess appeared at the supper table still flushed and breathless from her afternoon tryst with her host, she discovered herself quite unable to sit upon the chair being offered her.

'Difficulties, my dear?' queried the elderly gentleman beside her, his knowing smirk broadening beneath his mask as he used his napkin to flag down an attendant slave. To the countess's supreme humiliation, and before the amused eyes of all those who had gathered for the kitchen's offerings of cold soup, blood sausage and a succulent joint of beef, a special velvet cushion with a hollowed-out middle came to be provided for her by one of the slaves who served at table. Such alleviative equipment had become standard provision at the Castle, since it was very common for a guest to overindulge during a stay, especially at festival time. Even a leisurely stroll from her quarters to the dining room and back again afforded the countess great distress, the upward traversing of the stairs proving the most grievous ordeal. It was a miracle she could walk at all, for it felt as if someone had taken one of the fiery stakes that lighted the Castle corridors to the cheeks of her backside, to say nothing of her poor fundament.

The widow's ears continued to ring with the impassioned groans of the Martinet as he thrust into her bottom; a thrusting that seemed destined to continue until the end of time judging by the stiffness of his manhood. The countess had clenched and clenched the previously unused

walls of her anus to the point of fainting, hoping to squeeze
the hot juices of pleasure from her tormentor so he might
finally release her from his stabbing grip. But the only
effect her efforts had was to create further misery for
herself, for the Martinet had discharged so much of his
warm fluids inside her that they still trickled from her,
staining the back of her elegant festival gown and drawing
unwanted attention to her plight. To make matters worse,
as if they *could* have been any worse, the countess had
afterwards been unable to locate the dark-haired slave
girl who had for a generous fee fitted her with the
confining accoutrements she had initially been so keen to
wear for her planned seduction of the Martinet. The supple
straps of hide pulled vexingly upon the burning and
severely strained opening between her bruised bottom
cheeks. So too did the imprisoning rings of iron that had
been driven into the painfully throbbing wings of her
clitoris, the delicate flesh of which would surely tear if
something was not done at once to remove them. Oh,
whatever had she gotten herself into?

Alas, the countess's tearful laments would go unheard
by the one who had been the cause for them. Besides,
had it not been *she* who had beseeched her mysteriously
masked host to partake of her in this extremely unnatural
fashion? How she had burbled with laughter when it had
been another who suffered, especially when that other
happened to be the fair-haired and handsomely endowed
male slave who had been made into the paramour of the
Martinet's more deviant gentleman guests, including that
tottering brute of a Spaniard. However, unlike the
unfortunate soul whose shameful affliction she had on so
many occasions chuckled over, the countess could at least
be granted the dignity of her garments to cloak the gaping

evidence of her despoliation. All at once she surprised herself by the sudden wish that she could once again be the apathetic recipient of her late husband's amateur poking at the dry entrance of her womanhood rather than having possessed the folly to have placed her maiden fundament at the Herculean mercy of the Martinet's manhood.

Early the next morning, and without so much as a polite leave-taking directed towards her host, the Prussian countess was witnessed departing in her coach, her trunk laden with the fanciful garments she had so eagerly packed for festival week stored up top with the driver, who remained as ignorant of the contents as he was of the licentious goings-on behind the impenetrable walls of the Castle. She balanced with cringing care upon the inadequately padded banquette, facing fully forward, without so much as even daring to turn her regal head to glance back upon the place she was leaving.

It would appear the Martinet had gotten his way. The widow of the Prussian count would *not* be returning to the Castle, and threatening his bachelorhood, ever again.

The Festival of Saturnalia

With the timely and not altogether unanticipated departure
of his female guest, the Martinet could once again turn
his attention back to the important business at hand, namely
the festival. As an avid observer of human nature, each
year he found himself more and more astonished at just
how far some of his aristocratic visitors would go in their
pursuit of physical pleasure. Although it had always been
the custom to place very few limits upon those who came
to the Castle, these erotic merrymakers seemed to act
with particular intemperance during festival week,
indulging themselves in ways they would never before
have dared contemplate, and afterwards placing the blame
upon the strong blood-coloured Spanish wine that had
flowed all too freely into their happily proffered cups.
And the Martinet expected this year's festivities to be no
less dissolute, for his present crop of slaves possessed an
appeal that far outshone their predecessors'.

In addition to the Martinet's esteemed list of guests, it
had become an accepted tradition during the weeklong
celebration for slaves to be granted the license to revel as
well. This oftentimes consisted of an agreed-upon trading
of places between master and slave, where the master
served the slave, a radical change from the usual
commerce of sexual subservience that transpired at the
Castle on every other day of the year. Such an
unprecedented reversal of roles always provided much in
the way of entertainment to, and elicited little in the way

of protest from, the Martinet's distinguished callers, who discovered their newfound submission surprisingly pleasurable. To some this temporary fleshly servility toward another might lead to future such indulgences, resulting in the covert hiring away of slaves of tenure. Having themselves acted as masters of their enslaved underlings, they demonstrated the greatest capacity toward mastery, and these senior members of the slave hierarchy adjusted quite favourably to their new roles away from the Castle. As for the individual who hosted the yearly festivities that led to these events, the Martinet had always drawn a sharp line for himself he vowed never to cross when it came to this form of role reversal, considering it far too unseemly for a gentleman in his position. However, this year something had changed his mind.

That something was the beautiful young daughter of the English earl.

How many times had he observed her from across a room just as she, he believed, observed him... the quiescent eyes behind her black mask always seeming to ignite with a fiery passion whenever their gazes met... although this once haughty child of the nobility would cast them quickly downward with slave-like deference in the manner the former chambermaid who served as her trainer had instructed her to do. Annabella might have been able to hide the evidence of the desire burning in her eyes, but certain other evidence of her desire could not so easily be hidden.

Perhaps the greatest indicator of her secret feelings for the Martinet could be spied in the very palpable twitching upon their chains produced by the lustrous wings of her clitoris, which she, in hopes of gaining her handsome master's attention, had taken to liberally adorning with rouge, along with the smoothly barbered lips surrounding them. Under the stringent conditions set forth by Annabella's costume of enslavement, this amorous phenomenon would have been impossible to conceal from the Martinet's astute eye. Perhaps the Prussian countess had been correct after all; he *did* need a woman at his side.

Suddenly the blue-masked enigma who ruled at the Castle could think only of going onto his velvet-clad knees to serve the delicious apparition of the fair-fleshed and fair-haired slave girl who had already been made to serve so many. Aye, he would release those lusty flanges of sentient flesh from their iron-ringed bonds so his lips could feast upon their feminine sweetness. Of course, he would make certain to slip his nostalgic tongue into the accompanying spout below, just as he had seen his aristocratic female guests do with the soft moist centres of the rich honeyed desserts served at the supper table or, if she were thusly inclined, the soft moist centres of the Castle's more comely female slaves. For there were those who enjoyed the practice of tasting another of their gender, taking full advantage of the opportunity to satisfy this forbidden hunger now their identities were safely cloaked behind their masks. However, unlike these daring ladies of title, their host could not permit himself to do so publicly, although he might perhaps conduct such a transaction within the privacy of his chambers, where he could at last be free to experience what his own conventions had for too long denied him.

It had been years since the Martinet entertained such lusty thoughts; thoughts which kept him thrashing in his bed night after night, his tortured cries of 'Annabella! Annabella!' swallowed by the fluffy swan feathers stuffing his pillow. Under cover of darkness, he carefully staged his worship of the earl's daughter inside his head like the director of an elaborate play, savouring each detail of the performance. There were so many things he wished to do to her that he sometimes never got to sleep at all. For after the Martinet had completed his epicurean explorations of his favoured slave's conventional female parts he, without removing the functional bonds of hide forcing open the barbered cleft formed by the meeting of her fine English bottom cheeks, planned to turn the desirous attentions of his tongue to the much-lauded and advantageously stretched mouth of her fundament, the rouged charms of which so many gentlemen of the nobility had already enthusiastically sampled with their randy members. A man of meticulous habits, the Martinet would have dispatched Annabella beforehand to the Keeper of the Clyster to remove all traces of anyone having paid a social call before allowing his discriminating tongue to lose itself within the slave's fiery depths. In having so often found himself in the lonely blackness of night with his tongue thrusting desperately into a dream-induced thoroughfare, only to be left with the heartlessly sticky reality of bedclothes sodden with the liquid results of his illusionary passions, the Martinet expected *not* to be disappointed in the wakefulness of daylight.

With Annabella's fundament well primed with his saliva, the Martinet would have no need of any further lubricious condiments to aid his way. Thus he would continue with his journey by allowing the heretofore neglected shaft of his manhood to take a leisurely turn in her backside, sliding in and out of the tight trough with movements as gentle and loving as those that had been earlier undertaken by his tongue. However, unlike on previous occasions relegated to just another aspect of her training, this was to be an appetiser, a mere nibble of the divine feast to come. Although generally his preferred mode of erotic recreation, this time the Martinet wished to save up his strength for other matters. For despite such seeming diligence, there was still one more avenue of pleasure remaining for him to experience. Having methodically tasted the alternative delights of the earl's daughter, the Martinet would at last penetrate with his manhood the one entrance his gentlemen guests had always been forbidden from penetrating; the entrance of Annabella's womanhood. Only then would he make her his partner.

At last Annabella would be fully ready to take her place at his side, a readiness that had been even further enhanced by her having already passed muster with the Castle's most exacting trainer, the relentless Suzette. The Martinet knew well of the cruelty inflicted upon this delicate English flower courtesy of the marquis's former chambermaid. Nevertheless, it had been a cruelty of the utmost necessity, if he intended to successfully mould the earl's prideful daughter into a slave suitable for the cosmopolitan tastes of royalty, and likewise suitable for the cosmopolitan tastes the Martinet had also cultivated over a lifetime. During the months of Annabella's traineeship at the Castle, the Martinet had received numerous offers for the beautiful slave girl, offers put forth by men and women willing to part with what amounted to a king's ransom to procure this fair-fleshed young female of aristocratic heritage for their own personal courtesan. Even the lusty king of Spain himself had dispatched a subtle hint or two in his host's direction, which greatly surprised the Martinet, who anticipated that if such an imperial proposition were ever made it would surely have been intended for Prince

Tristam, since the Spanish king had always demonstrated a most vigorous fancy toward the handsome young man. Indeed, never in all his days had the Martinet seen a more frequented fundament as the one belonging to the English prince, a fact that obviously had a good deal to do with the licentious activities of the king. Yet by now the Martinet knew better than to ever be surprised by the actions of his guests, each of whom appeared determined to show one another up in their propensity toward debauchery.

Fortunately for everybody concerned, there would be debauchery aplenty once the Festival of Saturnalia got underway, some of which the Martinet intended to partake of himself with the earl's daughter. Thus far it was proving to be an unseasonably warm December, which would undoubtedly further heat the already well-fuelled passions of those in attendance. One might easily have wondered why so many trunks had ever been packed in the first place when their costly and fanciful costumes came to experience so little usage.

For in the seductive velvety warmth of the Spanish air, corsets and panniers would swiftly be discarded, as would be coats and breeches, although their titled owners continued to remain for the most part safely unidentified behind their special festival masks. As in previous years, these much-needed facial accessories had been designed to be even more elaborate for the occasion, with elegant braid trim and tiny rows of precious stones sewn into the lustrous Oriental satin or – for those in possession of somewhat more flamboyant natures, such as the recently gregarious Sir Percival – with sprigs of peacock feathers fanning out like giant eyebrows. It so happened the Martinet owned a similarly embellished mask in his trademark royal blue. Despite his reputation for never wearing the same costume more than once during festival week, the host of the festivities always found himself returning to his elaborately plumed festival mask. It provided a consistency during these seven days of sexual madness where it was most needed, making the Martinet easily identifiable among all the confusion and revelry, for he certainly did not wish to be mistaken for a slave who had temporarily donned the habiliment of his master.

Although highly useful to the Martinet, such predictability of costuming could have the unintended effect of being highly useful to others as well. Perhaps if he had not been so lustfully preoccupied with his own fantasies featuring the earl's beautiful daughter, the Martinet might have realised that the Castle's most popular male slave desired to place *himself* in the guise of master. However, rather than doing so with the eager acquiescence of a guest, this scheming slave of royal blood planned to do so with one equally as enslaved as himself. Still determined to regain what he could of his lost honour, the slave who endeavoured to embark upon this transitory change of roles was none other than Prince Tristam.

With the propitious arrival of festival week, the disgraced heir to the English throne knew that another occasion to procure the fleshly favours of the fair Annabella might never ever again come his way. Although he had no doubt the competition for her companionship would be keen, he had devised a very clever plan, a plan that placed considerable importance upon the Martinet's selection of a mask. In having chosen to don the more lavishly ornamented mask of festival time, the proprietor of the Castle had for the time being set aside his customary and simpler blue silk mask.

With his pierced and chained manhood already

shuddering with the imagined heat of Annabella's bottom, Prince Tristam decided to pay a stealthy call to the Martinet's private quarters, his intention being to claim the now unworn mask so he could replace his own slave-issue black with the elegant royal blue. To ensure the success of his venture, he cloaked the shameful bonds of his slavery beneath one of the costumes that had been made available to the Castle slaves for festival week. As for the matter of the most urgency, that being the vexingly inconvenient imprisonment of his manhood, Tristam's unfortunate nocturnal alliances with the felonious Frederico had inadvertently imparted upon him the knowledge of how to remove the ring of iron from the pierced flesh of his prepuce.

Naturally, such valuable knowledge did not come without a price. For in having provided his unwilling male paramour with what he most needed to know, the Spanish horse thief took cruel advantage of Tristam's temporary freedom by compelling him into a reciprocal arrangement. Hence, in order for the smitten prince to have the facility to pursue Annabella's patrician backside, he would be required to service the distinctly un-patrician buttocks of the man who had granted him his freedom: to service him in the same manner as that which he had so often been made to service the squealing Sir Percival. Yet even this was not so dear a price to pay for the brief acquisition of the fair-fleshed female slave whose brightly rouged fundament had haunted its enslaved royal admirer ever since he had witnessed its first clystering.

It was this very same lusty memory that prevented Prince Tristam from succumbing to madness as he thrust his mutinous member inside his swarthy liberator's tireless buttocks, closing his ears to the brutish masculine grunts his efforts inspired as he recalled instead the soft feminine whimpers of humiliation that played like the sweetest music inside his head. How deliciously the pink flush of shame had tainted Annabella's pale flesh as the leering Keeper administered his well-employed clyster to her fearfully uplifted bottom. Being there to witness it had been worth even Tristam's own humiliation; a humiliation most distressingly public as he sprayed his liquid excitement all over his heaving chest and belly before the eyes of the other slaves who had been summoned to the clystering chamber. And it quickly became evident from the expression in the masked eyes of the Castle's newest slave that she had witnessed her princely observer's pleasure, for such a frothy presentation could not have been mistaken for anything but. It was at this most telling of moments that Tristam knew he had to possess her, and to possess her in the manner most forbidden to a gentleman.

With Frederico's capricious passions momentarily sated – for with his deliverance into the sexual domain of men, Tristam had inadvertently become quite expert in the pleasuring of his own gender – the newly liberated royal would at last be able to seek out the fiery-bottomed female he wished to make his personal slave. Since many of the punitive restrictions placed upon Castle slaves had been relaxed during the Festival of Saturnalia, they too could pursue their desires, or at least pursue them to the degree in which their respective bonds permitted, the majority of the males having not been granted the license to remove their iron rings unless bidden by a guest or a slave of tenure to do so. For these slaves of common status who required the permission of their betters to release their imprisoned members, this did not seem at all just. Like the aristocratic personages they were required to serve, they could not blind themselves to the provocatively rouged charms of the Castle's female slaves or, for those of a particular persuasion, the Castle's male slaves.

Although they might not have been afforded the kind of freedom that allowed them to deny a guest's request for service, the slaves happily discovered they could at least be unaccountable for brief periods of time during the festivities without risk of punishment... which was exactly what Tristam had been counting on when he went in search of the Martinet's mask.

Unfortunately, the simple act of cloaking oneself in the guise of another does not necessarily guarantee the success of a venture. Such a masquerade did in fact guarantee Annabella's silent surrender of her much-coveted backside, yet no sooner had the prince managed to fit the gracefully arced shaft of his hungry manhood into the twinkling, rouged mouth of her anus than he discovered himself being interrupted by the real Martinet. Alas, Tristam would not be granted the long-awaited ecstasy of depositing his flowing appreciation inside these deliciously heated walls before he was ordered to unceremoniously withdraw from the luxurious haven and, in the process, was required to withstand the critical blue scrutiny of the master of the Castle. What transpired next would send a scorching spike of fear into young Tristam's gut, a spike that was simultaneously experienced in his unprotected backside.

'Hmm... perhaps thy member has been remiss in its duties,' mused the Martinet, his eyes narrowing menacingly behind his elaborately plumed festival mask. 'Aye, we must make certain that so impressive a specimen shall not be wasted in future.'

And with that, the English prince found himself being led away from the outthrust bottom whose sweet red mouth he had been so near to filling with his imperial seed. Which was probably just as well, for the Martinet's words, and the sinister meaning behind them, had by this time made Tristam incapable of filling anything. It was extremely rare for the Martinet to speak to a slave; when he did so, his words typically bode ill upon the one being addressed.

Had the enslaved young royal known the Martinet frequented the Castle courtyard during the afternoons when the Spanish sun was at its hottest and brightest, he would not have selected it as a place of seduction. Having observed the lone figure of Annabella making her determined way along the shadowy cloister, Tristam had availed himself of what appeared to be the perfect opportunity to follow her. It mattered not whether his much anticipated ravishment of her charming bottom took place indoors or out, but only that it took place. It was most unlikely that anyone should have desired to be outside in such uncompromising heat, a heat so intense it had turned the rich yellow fat Tristam had slathered upon his eager manhood into a slippery liquid.

Perhaps it was this very preparation that had acted against the hapless young prince and thereby summoned the unwanted presence of the Martinet. For the melted fat had added much in the way of mellifluousness to what proved to be an already mellifluous process within the enclosed echo chamber of the courtyard. The erotically cultured ear of the Martinet could not fail to decipher the distinctive music of such a transaction, especially when coupled with the groans of pleasure issuing forth from the throats of the earl's daughter and the king's son. In having spied the telltale flash of blue from a mask upon being seized from behind, Annabella had no reason to believe it was any but the Martinet's distinguished member engaged in the aggressive assault upon her fundament. Therefore, she had thrust her bottom willingly outward, bearing down on her innermost muscles to eagerly swallow the entire length of him.

Like her predecessor the Prussian countess, seduction had also been Annabella's plan when undertaking the bold action of visiting the courtyard. In fact, she had been very close to expressing her love for her handsome master when, without so much as a hint of warning, the burning and straining fullness she experienced in her buttocks suddenly ceased. Assuming with some disappointment that the Martinet had either finished prematurely or had not found her to his liking, she began to unfold herself from her servile crouch, only to recognise the voice of the Martinet coming from what sounded like a great distance behind her, his tense, angry tones seeming to be directed toward someone other than herself. Out of the corner of one eye – for Annabella had not as yet been given permission to turn her head – she saw what initially appeared to be *two* Martinets, except the one whose sadly dwindling manhood was positioned in close proximity to her nether cheeks had a small and very distinctive dot of pinkish-brown above his upper lip, a dot that could only have belonged to one man. But surely it could not have been...

Bitter tears filled Annabella's eyes as she came to realise the identity of the man who had just spent the last few minutes thrusting his member deeply inside her, a thrusting she had willingly offered herself up to, making no secret of the pleasure it gave her. Although she did not know

Tristam was a prince, Annabella knew he was a slave, the very same slave she had tried so often to avoid, for she did not like the salacious gleam in his eyes each time he looked at her. Never had she felt so naked and exposed as in those moments when they were together, when he served in his unwanted capacity as assistant, his knowing fingers meticulously greasing the entryway and interior of her bottom so that a Castle guest need not be sidetracked from taking his pleasure there. Granted, the earl's daughter might have been violated on a daily basis, but what had just transpired in the courtyard was a violation more heinous than any she had so far been subjected to in her entire time at the Castle. In Annabella's mind, she had been sullied. Perhaps the Martinet would not want her at all now. She would be blamed for what had happened, especially since she had done nothing but seem to encourage it.

Yet Annabella need not have worried about issues of blame. With his black slave's mask once again safely restored to his crestfallen face, Prince Tristam would be taken directly to the king of Spain, whose fancifully masked features brightened visibly at the sight of his favourite slave's unrestrained and generously greased manhood, which still retained some of its prior splendour as it projected out from his loins. Just before the thwarted young prince's arrival, the king and Sir Percival had been engaged in a temporary respite from the day's festivities over a chessboard. With the convenient appearance of the Castle's most popular male slave, an appearance inspired by the king's fortuitously timed shout of, 'Dispatch unto me the fair-headed lad!' the chess game was abandoned at once. A game with an altogether different strategy would now commence instead, a game in which the disguised heir to the English throne would be made into a pawn for both players.

Had Tristam only known of the fate that was very soon to befall him, he would have happily abandoned his plans to occupy Annabella's fundament. In fact, he would have thrown himself upon the mercy of his parents the king and queen, had it been possible for him to do so, begging for their forgiveness and the forgiveness of all those titled young ladies whose yielding bodies he had so callously used, and then forgotten. Yet instead he would find his life being forever changed by the Festival of Saturnalia and two of its celebrants.

This was the first time, although by no means the last, that Tristam would not only become the recipient of a gentleman's member, but also make another of his gender the simultaneous recipient of his own. So pleasing would this unique combination be to its pair of pleasure-seeking participants that the king of Spain and his chess playing associate devoted themselves to this felonious positioning for the whole remainder of festival week, deigning to accept no other slave into the snug and sweaty burrow between them but the well-favoured young Englishman. Alas, on these occasions his salacious fantasies of the fair-fleshed Annabella offered little in the way of comfort to Prince Tristam, and by the close of the day he found himself right back in the clutches of his swarthy bed-mate, who suddenly no longer cared to mute his pleasure from the amused ears of those who shared their intimate little slaves' quarters.

'A busy day has been enjoyed here, no?' teased the horse thief as he penetrated Tristam's smarting anus with one vicious plunge. Not surprisingly, Frederico would be extremely pleased to discover his enslaved companion well primed for a night's plundering, and he made the most of a convenient situation. He would even go so far as to offer his handsome prize to the two male slaves in the adjacent bed, both of whom declined the pleasure, preferring the plundering to be done to themselves rather than perpetrating it upon another themselves.

Having forfeited his temporary freedom by having had the folly to impose his will upon the one female slave in the entire Castle the Martinet had taken a fancy to, the discomfited prince would be powerless to prevent this further diminishment of his manliness. And it was a diminishment that became most distressingly public, for his shame at being used both to the fore and aft by those of his gender was voraciously witnessed by the mirthful eyes of any guest or slave who happened to be passing by. Shouts of encouragement were even put forth, inspiring the imposing royal figure behind Tristam to increase the vigorousness of his strokes, thereby prompting the disreputably sandwiched young heir to the throne into following suit with the flaccid backside before him while a crescendo of aristocratic laughter scorched his ears. Why, oh why, had he not paid heed to the gossip? For nearly everyone at the Castle had guessed the Martinet's interest in the flaxen-haired slave girl was no longer that of aloof master to slave – everyone by Tristam.

With each passing day of festival week, the hope that he might escape from the perverse clutches of the Spanish king and Sir Percival grew further distant. Like his unknown competitor, the Martinet, there had been so much more the English prince had planned to do when he finally succeeded in his quest to get the delicious daughter of the earl all to himself. In fact, her proposed ravishment had become an issue of even greater pride, what with his recent and unwanted embarkation into the exclusive sexual realm of men. Once it was all over, and she had turned to face her blue-masked lover, Tristam had intended to reveal his identity as the slave who had at every opportunity tormented her with his eyes and with his greased fingers. In the impetuous young royal's mind, such a disclosure would have been half the pleasure of possessing her, knowing as he did Annabella's personal distaste for his presence and, perhaps even most importantly, for his touch. Only instead of being allowed to fulfil his desires, Tristam was to be condemned to fulfilling the aberrant desires of other men, or at least to fulfilling them until the time of his sentence at the Castle had reached an end.

He wondered in despair if that time would ever come. And when it did, would he still be capable of attaining pleasure with a female, or would he have been so corrupted in his physical passions that he became one with those who had acted as his corrupters? *This* was what Prince Tristam feared the most – that he would one day ascend to the English throne as an aficionado of his own sex.

Although the Martinet could not find it in his heart to be too angry with the enterprising young slave for his foiled attempt to sample the lush pleasures of Annabella's sweet young buttocks, he needed to make certain such a sampling did not take place again, for the enslaved prince was not the only one at the Castle who had been smitten by her very agreeable charms. With his thoughts growing ever more covetous of the fair-fleshed daughter of the English earl, the Martinet knew he would be required to exercise considerable diplomacy in his efforts to remove the girl from the sexual domain of his guests, and to remove her with the utmost of subtlety so his actions did not draw any unwanted attention either to her or to himself, not to mention to his self-seeking reasons for doing so. Although he maintained a wealth of suitable replacements to offer his guests, there were always those stubborn few who had set their minds upon Annabella's charms and the greedy partaking of them, such as the ever-persistent Lady Rowena Campbell and her faithful friend, Lady Priscilla Bean. With this giggling pair of female conspirators dwelling beneath his roof, especially during the licentiousness of festival week, the Martinet had set quite a task for himself.

With the reliability of a Spanish sunrise, each time the two noblewomen paid a call to the Castle they would set about at once monopolising the earl's daughter. As secret fanciers of their own sex, Ladies Campbell and Bean could not be free to act upon their inclinations when dwelling beneath the restrictive roofs of their husbands, therefore they took it upon themselves to make up for their many long months of sexual drought by spending their precious days and nights at the Castle in delicious and anonymously masked self-indulgence, with the enticingly rouged Annabella serving as their shining lodestar. Oftentimes their slave of choice had not even been given the opportunity to claim her lute at supper before her comely presence was requested. No matter, for Lady Rowena and Lady Priscilla had other songs for the fair slave girl to sing, songs that required a greater complexity of verse and much plucking of cords, only these particular cords were constructed not from gut or fibre, but of needful clitoral flesh.

It might be assumed these two fine ladies of title should have chosen to assuage their special physical needs with one another, the opportunity to do so not being extraordinarily difficult for friends so dear as they. No one would have harboured a moment's suspicion if they had lingered a bit longer than usual over their pre-supper toilette before arriving at the table with their lips glossed and fragrant with the other's womanly juices. Safe and secure in their long held friendship, the feminine preparations of Lady Rowena Campbell and Lady Priscilla Bean did indeed include the clumsy insertion of a finger into the pinched mouth of a bashful fundament, or the unskilled lapping of a tongue against a hopeful clitoris. Regrettably, such forbidden and amateur ventures into the attainment of pleasure from one's own gender more often resulted in laughter and embarrassment than in any shudders of ecstasy.

'You silly, surely that is not the way to stimulate my clitty,' Lady Priscilla would squeal, slapping the other woman affectionately upon the top of her stiffly bobbing head.

'If you know so much about it, perhaps you ought to do it yourself,' retorted Lady Rowena, making as if to bite the rigid pink nib at her lips.

'And however might I do so, pray tell?' snapped Lady Priscilla, thrusting a dry finger into her friend's bottom with a palpable lack of tenderness, only to be countered with the sharp teeth that had been threatening. The interlude would inevitably conclude with a merry round of smacks upon the other's hind cheeks, that being the only form of stimulation the pair seemed qualified to perform.

Although a good deal could be blamed on inexperience, perhaps still more could be made of the fact that both Lady Rowena and Lady Priscilla simply did not fancy one another. Nevertheless, they most certainly fancied Annabella.

With all the ruthlessness of the notorious Rousseaulet the Highwayman, these refined ladies of title would have the Martinet's aristocratic slave flitting frenziedly from labial blossom to labial blossom, both of which had been positioned within easy reach of the other for the convenience of their female pleasure-giver and so that the fostering of their passions did not undergo any unnecessary delay. Like the bumblebee her actions so closely resembled, Annabella's well practiced tongue plunged deeply into these proffered gardens of fragrant womanhood, ferreting out the nectar seeping lustily from each fluid centre as the fleshy pink stamens above fluttered in long-awaited ecstasy.

With a markedly unladylike lewdness, both Lady Rowena and Lady Priscilla opened up the darkly furred lips of their sex with their fingertips in order for their slave of choice to perform a more thorough oral undertaking upon the distending flesh therein, leaving the earl's daughter no choice but to bow her head obediently within the deep V formed by each pair of widely parted thighs until both women were satisfied. It brought tears of shame to Annabella's eyes to think these two were ladies she and her father had very likely taken tea with in their stately home.

Yet for the earl's defamed daughter, there was a lot more shame to come. Even more unladylike would be the total lasciviousness with which these two callers to the Castle drew apart the elegantly rounded cheeks of their blue-blooded bottoms, opening themselves in ways they would never have done with their own husbands. This unscrupulous boldness would have shocked even a man as accustomed to these kinds of events as the Martinet, had he been present to witness it. In encountering the well-bred Lady Rowena Campbell and Lady Priscilla Bean at a social function, one would never have believed them capable of such stark lechery. However, here they were bending eagerly forward and exposing the daintily haired mouths of their fundaments to their captive female slave, whose accomplished tongue was expected to demonstrate the very same reverence that had been afforded these ladies' more traditional parts. And if this reverence proved in any way lacking, matters would quickly be set to rights with a stern admonishment by either Lady Rowena or Lady Priscilla, whose musical voices had by this time grown shrill with need as they endeavoured to emulate the formal speech of the Castle.

'Slave, dost not thy worthless tongue reach any deeper?' came the usual hysterical prompting, a prompting which would be responded to at once in the appropriately designated manner. For Annabella's training had made it clear to her that her sole function at the Castle was to provide pleasure in any form demanded of her, and with anyone who demanded it of her.

To the earl's enslaved daughter, the oral servicing of one aristocratic backside bore very little distinction to that of servicing another. Such activities had become routine for her, affording neither pleasure nor offence to their provider. As she had done earlier, Annabella flitted back and forth with equitable devotion between the two dark mouths being presented to her with such raw candour, having at last become acclimated to her role as Castle slave. Perhaps she had reached a kind of contentment, a placid acceptance of her new place in life. For no longer did the privileged young daughter of the English earl spend her days and nights lamenting tearfully upon the grave injustice of the sentence of humiliation imposed upon her by way of her unsuspecting father, who undoubtedly believed her to be in safe and wholesome hands. Over the weeks, she had come to learn she was really no different from any of the other young men and women who, because of some act of folly, had suddenly found themselves banished to this imposing stone fortress built by the Moors. As for when her length of imprisonment would end, that too mattered less and less to the punished Annabella. All that mattered to her was that she continued to please her blue-masked master by acting to please those who sought out her fleshly society, no matter the shame it brought her. If she continued to excel in her work, perhaps then he might truly acknowledge her...

Not a man typically disposed towards reflections of sympathy, even the stern figure of the Martinet could not fail to experience an element of pity for the overworked tongue of the earl's daughter, knowing as he did how thoroughly and intemperately it had likely been used to satisfy the greedy mounds and backsides belonging to Lady Rowena Campbell and Lady Priscilla Bean. Never had he encountered two women so seemingly incapable of exhaustion. They had been most candid with him during supper when discussing the superior oral talents of his highborn female slave, whom it was gleefully reported wielded a tongue as swift and sinuous as that of a serpent, a comment that inspired a surge of envy from their host, who did his best to hide his somewhat inhospitable feelings.

'Would you believe the naughty girl put her tongue in so far that it actually became stuck?' chortled Lady Rowena, the parts of her face not hidden by her mask flushing red with mirth. 'Why, we had to grease it with fat in order to pull it back out!'

'To be sure, the same thing happened with me!'

exclaimed Lady Priscilla, apparently not wanting to be left out of the merriment.

The Martinet joined in the laughter, although his resulted from far more than this graphic tale telling on behalf of his guests. This would not be the first time he had to refrain from the mischievous desire to inform these fine ladies of the nobility that they had made the charming acquaintance of this able-tongued female slave on numerous social occasions at the home of the English earl before his daughter's fall from grace with the viscount's son had led her to be enslaved at the Castle, and consequently enslaved by these ladies' gluttonous fundaments.

Although most of his guests considered their mysterious host impassive and without humour, it was precisely these kinds of coincidences that kept the Martinet happily entertained. If ever he decided to wreak havoc upon the aristocracy, all that would be required was for him to issue an order to the slaves to remove their black masks and the masks of their aristocratic partners, such an unveiling being employed at a moment of the utmost sexual compromise. There would not be a monarchy remaining in the whole of Europe once the participants of these scandalous liaisons were brought fully into the light.

However, such amusing prospects were of scant interest to the Martinet, who now had matters of much greater consequence to attend to. For with the Festival of Saturnalia in full swing, Lady Rowena Campbell and Lady Priscilla Bean would be given free and unabashed reign to reciprocate with their own inquisitive tongues upon Annabella's smoothly barbered and brightly rouged terrain. The sapphic duo had spoken of little else since their previous visit, this unprecedented reversal of roles proving as seductive to them as it did to their peers. Such prurient images as those that now tortured his similarly inclined thoughts would surely have driven the proprietor of the Castle to madness if he did not act in some way to prevent them from ever taking place.

Yet it would appear the Martinet was not the only one to be entertaining fantasies of prostrating himself before the divinely lovely daughter of the earl during the festival. The randy French viscount, who had partaken on so many lustful occasions of Annabella in a fashion denied to those of his ilk by the manners and dictates of court society, was also quite willing to fall onto his knees before the Castle's popular female slave. In fact, he had been loudly heard to remark after swallowing too many cups of wine at the supper table that there was no better time for such deliciously improper indulgences than during the days of festival. Unbeknownst to Annabella, the viscount happened to be none other than the father of the young man with whom she had so foolishly compromised herself, a compromise that had prompted her hasty dispatch to the Castle, and the placement of her malleable young body in the voracious hands of the Martinet's guests as well as in the even less tender hands of his senior slaves.

Attiring himself in a costume worthy of the most buffoonish of court jesters, the viscount would at last find himself worshipping at the rouged altar he had so often visited, and spent himself within. His heart thundered with the forbidden nature of his actions as he dared to allow his tongue to explore the luxurious dark depths that had previously been the domain of his member. If those of his society could have seen him or, as in the instance of those bearing witness to these unseemly events, *recognised* him, he would likely have been banished from ever again gracing their eminent doorsteps. Even his own son, whom the viscount had upbraided most harshly for his inappropriate association with the earl's young daughter, would have turned his head away in disgust at the public exhibition of his noble father salaciously thrusting his patrician tongue up the backside of a female slave. Ah, but how could a mere boy have known of such exotic pleasures, mused the viscount as the heat of Annabella's fundament scorched his probing tongue.

Had this French aristocrat not discovered the Castle, he too might have remained in unhappy ignorance.

Epilogue

As the guests in the boisterous spirit of the Festival of Saturnalia went on to satisfy their every secret whim by enslaving themselves to those whom they themselves had enslaved, the Martinet would be sequestered inside the privacy of his quarters, safely and contentedly far away from the hedonistic frolic taking place all around him. However, he did not find himself alone.

He had taken for his company the earl's daughter, who had silently presented herself at his door freshly barbered, clystered and rouged, and also very confused and frightened as to the reason why she had been summoned away from her duties. It was virtually unheard of for the Martinet to personally intervene in the activities of slaves, particularly during the demanding days of festival week, when not even the most illicit of fleshly enterprises was forbidden.

Although the Spanish sun still warmed the stone walls

of the Castle, a fire had been lit in the hearth, and its flames repeated themselves with blue similitude in the eyes behind the Martinet's gaily-plumed festival mask. As per slave etiquette, Annabella turned her anxious gaze towards the crackling logs rather than meeting that of her handsome master. In the glimpse of him she had stolen upon crossing the threshold, she had been unable to determine whether he contemplated her with passion or with menace. She wondered breathlessly if she had perchance committed some terrible wrong in her servitude at the Castle and was only now to suffer what would undoubtedly be the grievous consequences...

Yet Annabella could think of no possible wrongdoing, unless she was to be blamed for what had been the eager relinquishment of her fundament to the male slave who'd had the hubris to take on the mask of his master. Yet she had done so in perfect and trusting innocence, having believed her greased intruder to belong to the Martinet. Nay, it must have been some other transgression she had been found guilty of, a transgression involving a guest, although she could not think whom. The punished young daughter of the earl had denied no one, not even the hulking personage of the Spaniard who preferred the backsides of his own gender to those of females, although she had been bidden to painfully relinquish hers to the stately gentleman's prodigious member on a number of occasions, until the hindmost charms of a more masculine version of her enslaved self had fortunately been discovered, or at least fortunately for *her*.

Surely she could not be accused of neglecting the two ladies who always made so many rude demands upon her, demands their favoured slave laboured to meet, jumping to each scurrilous command like a trained animal performing in a travelling carnival, the taste of shame burning like a hot coal upon her thrusting and licking tongue. Could it be the Martinet had received some unjustified word of complaint from the older foreign gentleman whose syrupy manner of speech so reminded Annabella of her former beloved? Yet had she not submitted her bottom on enough occasions to the endless probing of this dreadful Frenchman's manhood and, indignity of indignities, the recent and likewise endless probing of his coarsely textured tongue? Such had been the viscount's aberrant desire the previous evening at supper as the Festival of Saturnalia got officially underway. Annabella had been forced in mid-verse to set aside her cherished lute so he could ravish the daughter of his societal foe before the attentive eyes of all, including even those of his host. The handsome features behind the Martinet's mask did not look at all pleased when the viscount urged his slave of choice forward over the table, until her rouged and ringed nipples had lain like two bonbons on his supper plate, only announce in a great boisterous tone that he desired to partake of a sweet the Castle kitchens had not seen fit to provide. And with no further fanfare, the French nobleman, who unbeknownst to his prostrate female victim claimed paternity for the young man with whom she had been so foolishly indiscreet in love, abruptly and unabashedly drove his thick tongue deep into the painted and accepting mouth of her bottom, eliciting from her an astonished squeal.

As Annabella's well employed fundament was forced to endure both public embarrassment and the rough surface of the viscount's unschooled tongue, which despite its inexperience, or perhaps because of it, demonstrated a propensity toward an irksome tenacity,

217

her eyes darted skittishly about the smoky torch-lit room, eventually connecting with those of the Martinet, whose distinctive blue irises were afire with an emotion akin to jealousy. Such a naked reaction from the impervious ruler of the Castle prompted a powerful shiver to course through her, a shiver the viscount apparently misconstrued as pleasure brought on by his activities in her nether regions. Reaching around with one hand, he began to rub at the pierced flanges of her clitoris as he exaggerated the crude thrusts of his tongue.

As this oral seduction of the viscount's favourite slave increased in its boldness, so too did the raucous reactions from the festively costumed onlookers who had gathered in a close circle to cheer him on in his pursuit. The most encouraging of these cheers came directly from the wicked lips of Lady Rowena and Lady Priscilla, who decided to offer the cheeks of Annabella's outthrust bottom a few friendly smacks of the palm, since they could not bear to be left out of the revelry.

'Naughty girl!' they scolded in unison, giggling with delight at the sound of flesh hitting flesh. They could barely keep from edging the portly figure of the viscount out of the way so they could have a go at the slave girl themselves.

When Annabella's aristocratic tormentor finally raised his head from his private banquet, his lips and chin were smeared with rouge. 'Very tasty,' he said, offering up a reddened smile of satisfaction to his table partners as well as to his distinguished host, who had not missed a moment of the lusty transaction.

It would be this very rouged smile that haunted the Martinet's sleep that night, as did the rowdy urgings of those he had so graciously opened his home to during these seven special days of erotic celebration. And he knew the viscount's leering red grin would haunt many more of his nights if he did not act swiftly to remove the earl's daughter from the coarse clutches of those who could not possibly appreciate, as did he, what so many weeks of meticulous grooming and training had resulted in. Had the Martinet not dispatched a senior slave to lead the girl away from the supper table, her defenceless backside would undoubtedly have been made the recipient of every tongue in the room, not to mention every male member. Although such a scenario might have once filled him with pride, it did so no longer. There were plenty of slaves at the Castle to keep his guests entertained during the Festival of Saturnalia; the absence of one slave should not make too great a difference.

With the flames in the hearth crackling their encouragement, the Martinet turned his attention to the fair female slave who stood shivering in fear before him. Forcing the clownishly costumed and red-lipped visage of the French viscount from his mind, the master of the Castle knelt down to remove the two tiny rings of iron from the forcefully elongated tips of Annabella's clitoris. His fingers trembled as he worked, for it had been only once before, and in entirely different circumstances, that he had been so close to this highborn slave's smoothly barbered and liberally rouged womanhood.

While deftly extricating the silken wings of flesh from their iron bonds, the Martinet suddenly discovered himself growing deliriously light-headed from the scent of their distinctive perfume. It had been a long time since he had allowed himself to indulge in these seemingly simple sensory pleasures. Not since the Lady Langtree affair, in fact.

However, with all due respect to her ladyship, never

had he experienced such a powerful emotion just from the mere glimpse of flesh, perfect pale flesh whose deliciously rouged parts he desired more than anything to explore with his tongue. Perhaps if the earl's daughter agreed to remain on at the Castle – for the time of her sentence was now at its end – he would make her his lady.

In the unadorned absence of the imprisoning rings of iron and their accompanying chains, the fleshy hood of Annabella's clitoris surged out towards its blue-masked liberator like a springtime flower coming into its first bloom. The red-hued tips, with their minutely bored holes, stood proudly away from the freshly pared nether lips that, thanks to the application of the chains, had long ago failed as cushions of modesty. The Martinet nodded with satisfaction; the ringed contraption had performed its work well. The ever-increasing tension of the two slender chains had permanently enlarged and aggrandised this delicate organ of sentient female flesh into an appendage of formidable magnitude. Although she might curse him now, for its appearance would have been shocking to anyone unaccustomed to the unique physical attributes of the Castle's female slaves, Annabella would one day come to appreciate what her guardian had done. Indeed, the refashioned contours of her newly unfettered clitoris would aid the earl's daughter well in her attainment of pleasure, the successful dispatching of which would henceforward require very little effort.

'Am I free, sire?' Annabella queried with tremulous humility, not daring to look down at her master's kneeling form, or at the flesh he had just released from its iron bonds.

'Only if thou wishes to be,' the Martinet replied softly,

his long-deprived tongue wet with the hot saliva of desire. And he observed kindred moisture emanating from the tiny pink slit now dwarfed by the voluminous blossom above, moisture that by its very nature had just given him the answer he sought. Heartened by this mellifluous manifestation of his slave's love for him, the Martinet removed from the little finger of his right hand the ruby ring he always wore, and slipped it reverently onto the finger of Annabella's hand traditionally designating wedlock. And then, with a joy unlike any he had ever experienced, the handsome and mysterious master of the Castle absorbed the liberated entirety of the Lady Annabella's clitoris into his mouth.

For she had truly become *his* lady.

More exciting titles available from Chimera

All **Chimera** titles are available from your local bookshop or newsagent, or direct from our mail order department. Please send your order with your credit card details, a cheque or postal order (made payable to *Chimera Publishing Ltd*) to: **Chimera Publishing Ltd., Readers' Services, PO Box 152, Waterlooville, Hants, PO8 9FS**. Or call our **24 hour telephone/fax credit card hotline: +44 (0)23 92 783037** (Visa, Mastercard, Switch, JCB and Solo only).

To order, send: Title, author, ISBN number and price for each book ordered, your full name and address, cheque or postal order for the total amount, and include the following for postage and packing:
UK and BFPO: £1.00 for the first book, and 50p for each additional book to a maximum of £3.50.
Overseas and Eire: £2.00 for the first book, £1.00 for the second and 50p for each additional book.

*Titles £5.99. **All others (latest releases) £6.99**

For a copy of our free catalogue please write to:

Chimera Publishing Ltd
Readers' Services
PO Box 152
Waterlooville
Hants
PO8 9FS

or email us at:
sales@chimerabooks.co.uk

or purchase from our range of superb titles at:
www.chimerabooks.co.uk

Sales and Distribution in the USA and Canada

Client Distribution Services, Inc
193 Edwards Drive
Jackson
TN 38301
USA
(800) 343 4499

Sales and Distribution in Australia

Dennis Jones & Associates Pty Ltd
19a Michellan Ct
Bayswater
Victoria
Australia 3153